Professor
Van Dusen

THE THINKING MACHINE

JACQUES FUTRELLE

D0088587

JOURNEY
FORTH™

Greenville, South Carolina

Library of Congress Cataloging-in-Publication Data

Futrelle, Jacques, 1875-1912.
    Professor Van Dusen : the thinking machine / by Jacques Futrelle.
    p. cm.
    ISBN 1-59166-384-9 (perfect bound pbk. : alk. paper)
  1. Van Dusen, Augustus S. F. X. (Fictitious character)—Fiction.
2. Detective and mystery stories, American. 3. College teachers—
Fiction. 4. Boston (Mass.)—Fiction. I. Title.
    PS3511.U97A6 2005
    813'.52—dc22

                                          2005009302

Design by Jamie Miller
Cover photo: PhotoDisc Inc./Getty Images
Composition by Michael Boone
© 2005 BJU Press
Greenville, SC 29614
Printed in the United States of America
ISBN 1-59166-384-9
15 14 13 12 11 10 9 8 7 6 5 4 3 2 1

Publisher's Note

American author Jacques Futrelle (1875-1912) was born in Georgia, and from his youth he worked in the newspaper business in a variety of capacities from printer's devil to telegraph editor.

In the early 1900s Futrelle spent two years as a writer, director, and actor in a Virginia theater. During this period of time he began developing his Thinking Machine stories. Eventually almost fifty stories featuring Professor Van Dusen appeared in serial form in magazines of the day and later in book-length collections.

In January of 1912 Jacques and his wife May traveled to Europe to visit publishers in an attempt to expand the European market for his novels and short stories. Their return trip to America was aboard the ill-fated maiden voyage of the RMS *Titanic*. While May survived the disaster and lived until 1967, Jacques perished at sea in April of 1912.

This Fingerprint Classic, *Professor Van Dusen: The Thinking Machine,* is a collection of Futrelle's short stories featuring the mental skills of the brilliant but crotchety scientist. The stories range from a prison escape in The Thinking Machine's most famous story, "The Problem of Cell 13," to the unmasking of a frightening apparition in "The Mystery of the Flaming Phantom." In every case, the fictional professor merely applies logic that is as simple—to him—as two plus two makes four.

Table of Contents

1

"THE THINKING MACHINE"

It was absolutely impossible.

Twenty-five chess masters from the world at large unanimously declared it impossible, and unanimity on any given point is unusual for chess masters. They were gathered in Boston for the annual championships, and not one would concede for an instant that it was within the range of human achievement. Some grew red in the face as they argued it. Others smiled loftily and were silent. Still others dismissed the matter in a word as wholly absurd.

A casual remark by the distinguished scientist and logician, Professor Augustus S. F. X. Van Dusen, had provoked the discussion. He had in the past aroused bitter disputes with some chance remark. In fact, he was often the center of controversy.

For many years educational and scientific institutions of the world had amused themselves by crowding degrees upon him. He had initials that stood for things he couldn't even pronounce— degrees from France, England, Russia, Germany, Italy, Sweden, and Spain. These expressed recognition of the fact that his was the foremost brain in the sciences. The imprint of his sullen personality lay heavily on half a dozen of its branches. Finally there came a time when argument was respectfully silent in the face of one of his conclusions.

The remark which had drawn the chess masters of the world into so formidable and unanimous a dissent was made by Professor Van Dusen in the presence of three other gentlemen of note. One of these, Dr. Charles Elbert, happened to be a chess enthusiast.

"Chess is a shameless perversion of the functions of the brain," was Professor Van Dusen's declaration in his perpetually irritated voice. "It is a sheer waste of effort, greater because it is possibly the most difficult of all fixed abstract problems. Of course, logic will solve it. Logic will solve any problem—not most of them, but *any* problem. A thorough understanding of the rules of chess would enable anyone to defeat your greatest chess players. It would be inevitable, just as inevitable as that two and two make four, not sometimes but all the time. I don't know chess because I never do useless things, but I could take a few hours of competent instruction and defeat a man who has devoted his life to it. His mind is cramped, bound down to the logic of chess. Mine is not; mine employs logic in its widest scope."

Dr. Elbert shook his head vigorously. "It is impossible," he asserted.

"Nothing is impossible," snapped the scientist. "The human mind can reason. It is what lifts us above the brute creation."

The aggressive tone and the uncompromising egotism brought a flush to Dr. Elbert's face. Professor Van Dusen affected many people that way, particularly those fellow scholars who, themselves men of distinction, had ideas of their own.

"Do you know the purposes of chess? Its countless combinations?" asked Dr. Elbert.

"No," was the surly reply. "I know nothing whatever of the game beyond the general purpose which I understand to be to move certain pieces in certain directions in order to stop an opponent from moving his King. Is that correct?"

"Yes," said Dr. Elbert slowly, "though I never heard it stated just that way before."

"Then if that is correct, I maintain that the true logician can defeat the chess expert by the pure mechanical rules of logic. I'll take a few hours some time, acquaint myself with the moves of the pieces, and defeat you to prove my point."

Professor Van Dusen glared savagely into the eyes of Dr. Elbert.

"Not me," said Dr. Elbert. "You said anyone. Would you be willing to meet the greatest chess player after you *acquaint* yourself with the game?"

"Certainly," said the scientist. "I have frequently found it necessary to make a fool of myself to convince people. I'll do it again."

This was the acrimonious beginning of the discussion which aroused the chess masters and brought open dissent from men who had never dared to dispute any assertion by the distinguished Professor Van Dusen.

It was arranged that at the conclusion of the annual championships, Professor Van Dusen would meet the winner. This happened to be Tschaikowsky, the Russian, who had been champion for half a dozen years.

After this expected result of the tournament, Hillsbury, a noted American master, spent a morning with Professor Van Dusen in his modest apartment on Beacon Hill. Hillsbury left there with a sadly puzzled face, and that afternoon Professor Van Dusen met the Russian champion. The newspapers had said a great deal about the affair, and hundreds were present to witness the game.

There was a little murmur of astonishment when Professor Van Dusen appeared. He was slight, almost child-like in body, and his thin shoulders seemed to droop beneath the weight of his enormous head. His brow rose straight and domelike, and a heavy shock of long, yellow hair gave him an almost grotesque appearance. His eyes were narrow slits of blue eternally squinting through thick spectacles. His face was small, clean shaven, drawn and white with the pallor of the student. His lips made a perfectly straight line. His hands were remarkable for their whiteness, their flexibility, and for the length of the slender fingers. One glance showed that physical development had never entered into the schedule of the scientist's fifty years of life.

The Russian smiled as he sat down at the chess table. He felt that he was humoring an eccentric. The other masters were grouped nearby, curiously expectant. Professor Van Dusen began the game, opening with a Queen's gambit. At his fifth move, made without the slightest hesitation, the smile left the Russian's face. At the tenth move, the masters grew intensely eager. The Russian champion was playing for honor now. Professor Van Dusen's fourteenth move was King's castle to Queen's four.

"Check," he announced.

After a long study of the board the Russian protected his King with a Knight. Professor Van Dusen noted the play then leaned back in his chair with finger tips pressed together. His eyes left the board and dreamily studied the ceiling. For at least ten minutes there was no sound, no movement, then, "Checkmate in fifteen moves," he said quietly.

There was a quick gasp of astonishment. It took the practiced eyes of the masters several minutes to verify the announcement. But the Russian champion saw and leaned back in his chair a little white and dazed. He was not astonished; he was helplessly floundering in a maze of incomprehensible things. Suddenly he arose and grasped the slender hand of his conqueror.

"You have never played chess before?" he asked.

"Never."

"You are not a man! You are a brain. A machine. A thinking machine!"

"It's a child's game," said the scientist abruptly. There was no note of exultation in his voice; it was still the irritable, impersonal tone which was habitual.

This was Professor Augustus S. F. X. Van Dusen, PhD, LLD, FRS, MD, et cetera, et cetera, et cetera, and this is how he came to be known to the world at large as The Thinking Machine.

The Russian's phrase was applied to the scientist as a title by a newspaper reporter, Hutchinson Hatch.

And it stuck.

2
THE PROBLEM OF CELL 13

I

It was only occasionally that The Thinking Machine had any visitors, and these were usually men who dropped in to argue a point. Two of these men, Dr. Charles Ransome and Alfred Fielding, called one evening to discuss some theory which is not of consequence here.

"Such a thing is impossible," declared Dr. Ransome in the course of the conversation.

"Nothing is impossible," declared The Thinking Machine with equal emphasis. He always spoke petulantly.

"How about the airship?" asked Dr. Ransome.

"That's not impossible at all," asserted The Thinking Machine. "It will be invented some time. I would do it myself, but I'm busy."

Dr. Ransome laughed tolerantly.

"I've heard you say such things before," he said. "But they mean nothing. Mind may be master of matter, but it hasn't yet found a way to apply itself. There are some things which would not yield to any amount of thinking."

"What, for instance?" demanded The Thinking Machine.

Dr. Ransome was thoughtful for a moment.

"Well, say prison walls," he replied. "No man can think himself out of a cell. If he could, there would be no prisoners."

"A man can so apply his brain and ingenuity that he can leave a cell, which is the same thing," snapped The Thinking Machine.

Dr. Ransome was slightly amused.

"Let's imagine a case," he said, after a moment. "Take a cell where prisoners under sentence of death are confined—men who are desperate and, maddened by fear, would take any chance to escape. Suppose you were locked in such a cell. Could you escape?"

"Certainly," declared The Thinking Machine.

"Of course," said Mr. Fielding, who entered the conversation for the first time, "you might wreck the cell with an explosive, but if you were a prisoner, you wouldn't have that option."

"It would require nothing of that kind," said The Thinking Machine. "You could treat me precisely as you treat all prisoners under sentence of death, and I would leave the cell."

"Not unless you entered it with tools prepared to get out," said Dr. Ransome.

The Thinking Machine was visibly annoyed, and his blue eyes snapped.

"Lock me in any cell in any prison anywhere at any time, wearing only what is necessary, and I'll escape in a week," he declared sharply.

Dr. Ransome sat up straight in the chair, interested.

"You mean you could actually *think* yourself out?" asked Dr. Ransome.

"I would get out," was the response.

"Are you serious?"

"Certainly I am serious."

Dr. Ransome and Mr. Fielding were silent for a long time.

"Would you be willing to try it?" asked Mr. Fielding finally.

"Certainly," said Professor Van Dusen, and there was a trace of irony in his voice. "I have done more asinine things than that to convince other men of less important truths."

The tone was offensive, and there was an undercurrent strongly resembling anger on both sides. Of course, it was an absurd thing, but Professor Van Dusen reiterated his willingness to undertake the escape, and it was decided upon.

"We'll begin now," said Dr. Ransome.

"I'd prefer that it begin tomorrow," said The Thinking Machine, "because—"

"No, now," said Mr. Fielding, flatly. "You are arrested—figuratively, of course—without any warning, locked in a cell with no chance to communicate with friends, and left there with exactly the same care and attention that would be given to a man under sentence of death. Are you willing?"

"All right. Now, then," said the Thinking Machine, and he arose.

"Say, the death cell in Chisholm Prison."

"The death cell in Chisholm Prison."

"And what will you wear?"

"As little as possible," said The Thinking Machine. "Shoes, stockings, trousers, and a shirt."

"You will permit yourself to be searched, of course?"

"I am to be treated precisely as all prisoners are treated," said The Thinking Machine. "No more attention and no less."

There were some preliminaries to be arranged in the matter of obtaining permission for the test, but all three were influential men and everything was done satisfactorily by telephone, albeit the prison commissioners, to whom the experiment was explained on purely scientific grounds, were sadly bewildered. Professor Van Dusen would be the most distinguished prisoner they had ever entertained.

When The Thinking Machine had donned those things which he was to wear during his incarceration, he called the little old woman who was his housekeeper, cook, and maidservant all in one.

"Martha," he said, "it is now twenty-seven minutes past nine o'clock. I am going away. One week from tonight, at half-past nine, these gentlemen and one, possibly two, others will take supper with me here. Remember Dr. Ransome is very fond of artichokes."

The three men were driven to Chisholm Prison, where the warden was awaiting them. He had been informed of the matter by telephone. He understood merely that the eminent Professor Van Dusen was to be his prisoner—if he could keep him—for one week, that he had committed no crime, but that he was to be treated as all other prisoners were treated.

"Search him," instructed Dr. Ransome.

The Thinking Machine was searched. Nothing was found on him; the pockets of the trousers were empty; the white, stiffly starched shirt had no pocket. The shoes and stockings were removed, examined, then replaced. As he watched all these preliminaries— the rigid search; the pitiful, childlike physical weakness of the man; the colorless face; and the thin, white hands—Dr. Ransome almost regretted his part in the affair.

"Are you sure you want to do this?" he asked.

"Would you be convinced if I did not?" inquired The Thinking Machine in turn.

"No."

"All right. I'll do it."

What sympathy Dr. Ransome had was dispelled by the tone. It nettled him, and he resolved to see the experiment to the end. It would be a stinging reproof to egotism.

"It will be impossible for him to communicate with anyone outside?" he asked.

"Absolutely impossible," replied the warden. "He will not be permitted writing materials of any sort."

"And your jailers? Would they deliver a message from him?"

"Not one word, directly or indirectly," said the warden. "You may rest assured of that. They will report anything he might say or turn over to me anything he might give them."

"That seems entirely satisfactory," said Mr. Fielding, who was frankly interested in the problem.

"Of course, in the event he fails," said Dr. Ransome, "and asks for his liberty, you understand you are to set him free?"

"I understand," replied the warden.

The Thinking Machine stood listening but had nothing to say until this was all ended. "I should like to make three small requests. You may grant them or not, as you wish."

"No special favors, now," warned Mr. Fielding.

"I am asking none," was the stiff response. "I would like to have some tooth powder—buy it yourself to see that it is tooth powder—and I should like to have one five-dollar and two ten-dollar bills."

Dr. Ransome, Mr. Fielding, and the warden all exchanged astonished glances. They were not surprised at the request for tooth powder but were at the request for money.

"Is there any man with whom our friend would come in contact that he could bribe with twenty-five dollars?" asked Dr. Ransome of the warden.

"Not for twenty-five *hundred* dollars," was the positive reply.

"Well, let him have them," said Mr. Fielding. "I think they are harmless enough."

"And what is the third request?" asked Dr. Ransome.

"I should like to have my shoes polished."

Again the astonished glances were exchanged. This last request was the height of absurdity, so they agreed to it. These things all being attended to, The Thinking Machine was led back into the prison from which he had undertaken to escape.

"Here is Cell 13," said the warden, stopping three doors down the steel corridor. "This is where we keep condemned murderers.

No one can leave it without my permission, and no one in it can communicate with the outside. I'll stake my reputation on that. It's only three doors back of my office, and I can readily hear any unusual noise."

"Will this cell do, gentlemen?" asked The Thinking Machine. There was a touch of irony in his voice.

"Admirably," was the reply.

The heavy steel door was thrown open. There was a great scurrying and scampering of tiny feet, and The Thinking Machine passed into the gloom of the cell. Then the door was closed and double locked by the warden.

"What is that noise in there?" asked Dr. Ransome, through the bars.

"Rats—dozens of them," replied The Thinking Machine, tersely.

The three men, with final good nights, were turning away when The Thinking Machine called, "What time is it exactly, warden?"

"Eleven seventeen," replied the warden.

"Thanks. I will join you gentlemen in your office at half-past eight o'clock one week from tonight," said The Thinking Machine.

"And if you do not?"

"There is no *if* about it."

II

Chisholm Prison was a great sprawling structure of granite— four stories in all—which stood in the center of acres of open space. It was surrounded by a wall of solid masonry eighteen feet high, and so smoothly finished inside and out as to offer no foothold to a climber, no matter how expert. Atop of this fence, as a further precaution, was a five-foot fence of steel rods, each terminating in a keen point. This fence in itself marked an absolute demarcation between freedom and imprisonment, for even if a man escaped from his cell, it would seem impossible for him to cross the wall.

The yard was twenty-five feet from the building to the wall on all sides of the prison building. It was by day an exercise ground for those prisoners to whom was granted the boon of occasional semi-liberty. But there was no liberty for those in Cell 13. At all times of the day there were armed guards in the yard, four of them, one patrolling each side of the prison building.

By night the yard was almost as brilliantly lighted as by day. On each of the four sides was a great light which rose above the prison wall and gave the guards a clear sight and brightly illuminated the spiked top of the wall. The wires which fed the lights ran up the side of the prison building on insulators and from the top story led out to the poles supporting the electric lights.

All these things were seen and comprehended by The Thinking Machine, who was enabled to see out his closely barred cell window only by standing on his bed. This he did on the morning following his incarceration. He gathered, too, that the river lay over there beyond the wall somewhere, because he heard faintly the pulsation of a motor boat and high up in the air saw a river bird. From that same direction came the shouts of boys at play and the occasional crack of a batted ball. He knew then that between the prison wall and the river was an open space—a playground.

Chisholm Prison was regarded as absolutely safe. No man had ever escaped from it. The Thinking Machine, from his perch on the bed, seeing what he saw, could readily understand why. The walls of the cell, though built he judged twenty years before, were perfectly solid. The window bars of new iron had not a shadow of rust on them. The window itself, even with the bars out, would be a difficult mode of egress because it was small.

Yet seeing these things, The Thinking Machine was not discouraged. Instead, he thoughtfully squinted at the great light—in the bright sunlight—and traced with his eyes the wire which led from it to the building. That electric wire, he reasoned, must come down the side of the building not a great distance from his cell. That might be worth knowing.

Cell 13 was on the same floor with the offices of the prison, that is, not in the basement or even upstairs. There were only four steps up to the office floor, therefore the level of the floor must be only three or four feet above the ground. He couldn't see the ground directly beneath his window, but he could see it further out toward the wall. It would be an easy drop from the window. Well and good.

Then The Thinking Machine fell to remembering how he had come to the cell. First, there was the outside guard's booth in a part of the wall. There were two heavily barred gates there, both of steel. At this gate one man was always on guard. He admitted persons to the prison after much clanking of keys and locks, and let them out when ordered to do so. The warden's office was in the prison building, and in order to reach that official from the prison yard one had to pass a gate of solid steel with only a peephole in it. Then coming from that inner office to Cell 13, where he was now, one must pass a heavy wooden door and two steel doors into the corridors of the prison, and always there was the double-locked door of Cell 13 to reckon with.

So there were then seven doors to be overcome before one could pass from Cell 13 into the outer world, a free man. But against this was the fact that The Thinking Machine was rarely interrupted. A jailer appeared at his cell door at six in the morning with a breakfast of prison fare; he would come again at noon, and again at six in the afternoon. At nine o'clock at night would come the inspection tour. That would be all.

It's admirably arranged, this prison system, was the mental tribute paid by The Thinking Machine. *I'll have to study it a little when I get out. I had no idea there was such great care exercised in the prisons.*

There was nothing, positively nothing, in his cell, except his iron bed, so firmly put together that no man could tear it to pieces save with sledges or a file. He had neither of these. There was not even a chair, or a small table, or a bit of tin or crockery. Nothing. The jailer stood by when he ate and then took away the wooden spoon and bowl which he had used.

One by one these things sank into the brain of The Thinking Machine. When the last possibility had been considered, he began an examination of his cell. From the roof, down the walls on all sides, he examined the stones and the cement between them. He stamped over the floor carefully time after time, but it was cement, perfectly solid. After the examination he sat on the edge of the iron bed and was lost in thought for a long time. For Professor Augustus S. F. X. Van Dusen, The Thinking Machine, had something to think about.

He was disturbed by a rat, which ran across his foot and then scampered away into a dark corner of the cell, frightened at its own daring. After awhile The Thinking Machine, squinting steadily into the darkness of the corner where the rat had gone, was able to make out in the gloom many little beady eyes staring at him. He counted six pair, and there were perhaps others; he didn't see very well.

Then The Thinking Machine, from his seat on the bed, noticed for the first time the bottom of his cell door. There was an opening there of two inches between the steel bar and the floor. Still looking steadily at this opening, The Thinking Machine backed suddenly into the corner where he had seen the beady eyes. There was a great scampering of tiny feet, several squeaks of frightened rodents, and then silence.

None of the rats had gone out the door, yet there were none in the cell. Therefore there must be another way out of the cell, however small. The Thinking Machine, on hands and knees, started a search for this spot, feeling in the darkness with his long, slender fingers.

At last his search was rewarded. He came upon a small opening in the floor, level with the cement. It was perfectly round and larger than a silver dollar. This was the way the rats had gone. He put his fingers deep into the opening; it seemed to be an unused drainage pipe and was dry and dusty.

Having satisfied himself on this point, he sat on the bed again for an hour and then made another inspection of his surroundings through the small cell window. One of the outside guards stood directly opposite, beside the wall, and happened to be looking at the window of Cell 13 when the head of The Thinking Machine appeared. But the scientist didn't notice the guard.

Noon came, and the jailer appeared with the prison dinner of repulsively plain food. At home The Thinking Machine merely ate to live; here he took what was offered without comment. Occasionally he spoke to the jailer who stood outside the door watching him.

"Any improvements made here in the last few years?" he asked.

"Nothing particularly," replied the jailer. "New wall was built four years ago."

"Anything done to the prison proper?"

"Painted the woodwork outside, and I believe about seven years ago a new system of plumbing was put in."

"Ah!" said the prisoner. "How far is the river over there?"

"About three hundred feet. The boys have a baseball ground between the wall and the river."

The Thinking Machine had nothing further to say just then, but when the jailer was ready to go, he asked for some water.

"I get very thirsty here," he explained. "Would it be possible for you to leave a little water in a bowl for me?"

"I'll ask the warden," replied the jailer, and he went away. Half an hour later he returned with water in a small earthen bowl.

"The warden says you may keep this bowl," he informed the prisoner. "But you must show it to me when I ask for it. If it is broken, it will be the last."

"Thank you," said The Thinking Machine. "I shan't break it."

The jailer went on about his duties. For just the fraction of a second it seemed that The Thinking Machine wanted to ask a question, but he didn't.

Two hours later this same jailer, in passing the door of Cell Number 13, heard a noise inside and stopped. The Thinking Machine was down on his hands and knees in a corner of the cell, and from that same corner came several frightened squeaks. The jailer looked on interestedly.

"Ah, I've got you," he heard the prisoner say.

14

"Got what?" he asked, sharply.

"One of these rats," was the reply. "See?" And between the scientist's long fingers the jailer saw a small gray rat struggling. The prisoner brought it over to the light and looked at it closely. "It's a water rat," he said.

"Ain't you got anything better to do than to catch rats?" asked the jailer.

"It's disgraceful that they should be here at all," was the irritated reply. "Take this one away and kill it. There are dozens more where it came from."

The jailer took the wriggling, squirmy rodent and flung it down on the floor violently. It gave one squeak and lay still. Later he reported the incident to the warden, who only smiled.

Still later that afternoon the outside armed guard on the Cell 13 side of the prison looked up again at the window and saw the prisoner looking out. He saw a hand raised to the barred window and then something white fluttered to the ground, directly under the window of Cell 13. It was a little roll of linen, evidently of white shirting material, and tied around it was a five-dollar bill. The guard looked up at the window again, but the face had disappeared.

With a grim smile he took the little linen roll and the five-dollar bill to the warden's office. There together they deciphered something which was written on it with a queer sort of ink, frequently blurred. On the outside was this:

Finder of this please deliver to Dr. Charles Ransome.

"Ah," said the warden, with a chuckle. "Plan of escape number one has gone wrong." Then, as an afterthought, "But why did he address it to Dr. Ransome?"

"And where did he get the pen and ink to write with?" asked the guard.

The warden looked at the guard, and the guard looked at the warden. There was no apparent solution to that mystery. The warden studied the writing carefully and then shook his head.

"Well, let's see what he was going to say to Dr. Ransome," he said at length, still puzzled, and he unrolled the inner piece of linen.

"Well, if that . . . what . . . what do you think of that?" he asked, dazed.

The guard took the bit of linen and read this:

Epa cseot d'net niiy awe htto n'si sih. T.

III

The warden spent an hour wondering what sort of a cipher it was, and half an hour wondering why his prisoner should attempt to communicate with Dr. Ransome, who was the cause of him being there. After this the warden devoted some thought to the question of where the prisoner got writing materials and what sort of writing materials he had. With the idea of illuminating this point, he examined the linen again. It was a torn part of a white shirt and had ragged edges.

Now it was possible to account for the linen, but what the prisoner had used to write with was another matter. The warden knew it would have been impossible for him to have either a pen or a pencil, but neither pen nor pencil had been used in this writing. What, then? The warden decided to personally investigate. The Thinking Machine was his prisoner; he had orders to hold his prisoners; if this one sought to escape by sending cipher messages to persons outside, he would stop it, as he would have stopped it in the case of any other prisoner.

The warden went back to Cell 13 and found The Thinking Machine on his hands and knees on the floor, engaged in nothing more alarming than catching rats. The prisoner heard the warden's step and turned to him quickly.

"It's disgraceful," he snapped, "these rats. There are scores of them."

"Other men have been able to stand them," said the warden. "Here is another shirt for you. Let me have the one you have on."

"Why?" demanded The Thinking Machine, quickly. His tone was hardly natural, his manner suggested actual agitation.

"You have attempted to communicate with Dr. Ransome," said the warden severely. "As my prisoner, it is my duty to put a stop to it."

The Thinking Machine was silent for a moment.

"All right," he said, finally. "Do your duty."

The warden smiled grimly. The prisoner arose from the floor and removed the white shirt, putting on instead a striped convict shirt the warden had brought. The warden took the white shirt from him eagerly, and then there compared the pieces of linen on which was written the cipher with certain torn places in the shirt. The Thinking Machine looked on curiously.

"The guard brought you those, then?" he asked.

"He certainly did," replied the warden triumphantly. "And that ends your first attempt to escape."

The Thinking Machine watched the warden as he, by comparison, established to his own satisfaction that only two pieces of linen had been torn from the white shirt.

"What did you write this with?" demanded the warden.

"I should think it a part of your duty to find out," said The Thinking Machine irritably.

The warden started to say some harsh things, then restrained himself, and made a minute search of the cell and of the prisoner instead. He found absolutely nothing; not even a match or toothpick which might have been used for a pen. The same mystery surrounded the fluid with which the cipher had been written. Although the warden left Cell 13 visibly annoyed, he took the torn shirt in triumph.

"Well, writing notes on a shirt won't get him out, that's certain," he told himself with some complacency. He put the linen scraps into his desk to await developments. "If that man escapes from that cell, I'll . . . I'll resign."

On the third day of his incarceration The Thinking Machine openly attempted to bribe his way out. The jailer had brought his dinner and was leaning against the barred door waiting when The Thinking Machine began the conversation.

"The drainage pipes of the prison lead to the river, don't they?" he asked.

"Yes," said the jailer.

"I suppose they are very small?"

"Too small to crawl through if that's what you're thinking about," was the grinning response.

There was silence until The Thinking Machine finished his meal. Then, "You know I'm not a criminal, don't you?"

"Yes."

"And that I've a perfect right to be freed if I demand it?"

"Yes."

"Well, I came here believing that I could make my escape," said the prisoner, and his squinting eyes studied the face of the jailer. "Would you consider a financial reward for aiding me to escape?"

The jailer, who happened to be an honest man, looked at the slender, weak figure of the prisoner, at the large head with its mass of yellow hair, and he was almost sorry.

"I guess prisons like these were not built for the likes of you to get out of," he said at last.

"But would you consider a proposition to help me get out?" the prisoner insisted, almost beseechingly.

"No," said the jailer, shortly.

"Five hundred dollars," urged The Thinking Machine. "I am not a criminal."

"No," said the jailer.

"A thousand?"

"No," again said the jailer, and he started away hurriedly to escape further temptation. Then he turned back. "If you gave me ten thousand dollars, I couldn't get you out. You'd have to pass through seven doors, and I only have the keys to two."

Then he told the warden all about it.

"Plan number two fails," said the warden, smiling grimly. "First a cipher, then bribery."

When the jailer was on his way to Cell 13 at six o'clock, again bearing food to The Thinking Machine, he paused, startled by the unmistakable *scrape, scrape* of steel against steel. It stopped at the sound of his steps, then craftily the jailer, who was beyond the prisoner's range of vision, resumed his tramping, the sound being apparently that of a man going away from Cell 13. As a matter of fact he was in the same spot.

After a moment there came again the steady *scrape, scrape,* and the jailer crept cautiously on tiptoes to the door and peered between the bars. The Thinking Machine was standing on the iron bed working at the bars of the little window. He was using a file, judging from the backward and forward swing of his arms.

Cautiously the jailer crept back to the office, summoned the warden in person, and they returned to Cell 13 on tiptoes. The steady scrape was still audible. The warden listened to satisfy himself and then suddenly appeared at the door.

"Well?" he demanded, and there was a smile on his face.

The Thinking Machine glanced back from his perch on the bed and leaped suddenly to the floor, making frantic efforts to hide something. The warden went in, with hand extended.

"Give it up," he said.

"No," said the prisoner, sharply.

"Come, give it up," urged the warden." I don't want to have to search you again."

"No," repeated the prisoner.

"What was it, a file?" asked the warden.

The Thinking Machine was silent and stood squinting at the warden with something very nearly approaching disappointment on his face—nearly, but not quite. The warden was almost sympathetic.

"Plan number three fails, eh?" he asked, good-naturedly. "Too bad, isn't it?"

The prisoner didn't say.

"Search him," instructed the warden.

The jailer searched the prisoner carefully. At last, artfully concealed in the waistband of the trousers, he found a piece of steel about two inches long, with one side curved like a half moon.

"Ah," said the warden, as he received it from the jailer. "From your shoe heel," and he smiled pleasantly.

The jailer continued his search and on the other side of the trousers waistband found another piece of steel identical with the first. The edges showed where they had been worn against the bars of the window.

"You couldn't saw a way through those bars with these," said the warden.

"I could have," said The Thinking Machine firmly.

"In six months, perhaps," said the warden, good-naturedly.

The warden shook his head slowly as he gazed into the slightly flushed face of his prisoner. "Ready to give it up?" he asked.

"I haven't started yet," was the prompt reply.

Then came another exhaustive search of the cell. Carefully the two men went over it, finally turning out the bed and searching that. Nothing. The warden in person climbed upon the bed and examined the bars of the window where the prisoner had been sawing. When he looked, he was amused.

"Just made it a little bright by hard rubbing," he said to the prisoner, who stood looking on with a somewhat crestfallen air. The warden grasped the iron bars in his strong hands and tried to shake them. They were immovable, set firmly in the solid granite. He examined each in turn and found them all satisfactory. Finally he climbed down from the bed.

"Give it up, professor," he advised.

The Thinking Machine shook his head, and the warden and jailer passed on again. As they disappeared down the corridor, The Thinking Machine sat on the edge of the bed with his head in his hands.

"He's crazy to try to get out of that cell," commented the jailer.

"Of course, he can't get out," said the warden. "But he's clever. I would like to know what he wrote that cipher with."

It was four o'clock next morning when an awful, heart-racking shriek of terror resounded through the great prison. It came from a cell somewhere about the center, and its tone told a tale of horror, agony, and terrible fear. The warden heard and with three of his men rushed into the long corridor leading to Cell 13.

IV

As they ran there came again that awful cry. It died away in a sort of wail. The white faces of prisoners appeared at cell doors upstairs and down, staring out wonderingly, frightened.

"It's that fool in Cell 13," grumbled the warden.

He stopped and stared in as one of the jailers flashed a lantern. That "fool in Cell 13" lay comfortably on his cot, flat on his back with his mouth open, snoring. Even as they looked there came again the piercing cry, from somewhere above. The warden's face blanched a little as he started up the stairs. There on the top floor he found a man in Cell 43, directly above Cell 13, but two floors higher, cowering in a corner of his cell.

"What's the matter?" demanded the warden.

"You've come," exclaimed the prisoner, and he cast himself against the bars of his cell.

"What is it?" demanded the warden again.

He threw open the door and went in. The prisoner dropped on his knees and clasped the warden about the body. His face was

21

white with terror, his eyes were widely distended, and he was shuddering. His hands, icy cold, clutched at the warden's.

"Take me out of this cell, please take me out," he pleaded.

"What's the matter with you, anyhow?" insisted the warden, impatiently.

"I heard something—something," said the prisoner, and his eyes roved nervously around the cell.

"What did you hear?"

"I . . . I can't tell you," stammered the prisoner. Then, in a sudden burst of terror: "Take me out of this cell! Put me anywhere, but take me out of here."

The warden and the three jailers exchanged glances.

"Who is this fellow? What's he accused of?" asked the warden.

"Joseph Ballard," said one of the jailers. "He's accused of throwing acid in a woman's face. She died from it."

"But they can't prove it," gasped the prisoner. "They can't prove it. Please put me in some other cell."

He was still clinging to the warden, who threw the man's arms off roughly. Then for a time he stood looking at the cowering wretch, who seemed possessed of all the wild, unreasoning terror of a child.

"Look here, Ballard," said the warden, finally, "if you heard anything, I want to know what it was. Now tell me."

"I can't, I can't," was the reply. He was sobbing.

"Where did it come from?"

"I don't know. Everywhere. Nowhere. I just heard it."

"What was it . . . a voice?"

"Please don't make me answer," pleaded the prisoner.

"You must answer," said the warden, sharply.

"It was a voice, but . . . but it wasn't human," was the sobbing reply.

"Voice, but not human?" repeated the warden, puzzled.

"It sounded muffled and . . . and far away . . . and ghostly," explained the man.

"Did it come from inside or outside the prison?"

"It didn't seem to come from anywhere. It was just here. Here. Everywhere. I heard it. I heard it."

For an hour the warden tried to get the story, but Ballard had become suddenly obstinate and would say nothing, only pleaded to be placed in another cell, or to have one of the jailers remain near him until daylight. These requests were gruffly refused.

"And see here," said the warden, in conclusion, "if there's any more of this screaming, I'll put you in the padded cell."

Then the warden went his way, a sadly puzzled man. Ballard sat at his cell door until daylight, his face, drawn and white with terror, pressed against the bars, and looked out into the prison with wide, staring eyes.

That day, the fourth since the incarceration of The Thinking Machine, was enlivened considerably by the volunteer prisoner, who spent most of his time at the little window of his cell. He began proceedings by throwing another piece of linen down to the guard, who picked it up dutifully and took it to the warden. On it was written:

Only three days more.

The warden was in no way surprised at what he read; he understood that The Thinking Machine meant only three days more of his imprisonment, and he regarded the note as a boast. But how was the thing written? Where had The Thinking Machine found this new piece of linen? Where? How? He carefully examined the linen. It was white finely textured shirting material. He took the shirt which he had taken and carefully fitted the two original pieces of the linen to the torn places. This third piece didn't fit anywhere, and yet it was unmistakably the same goods.

"And where . . . where does he get anything to write with?" demanded the warden of the world at large.

Still later on the fourth day The Thinking Machine, through the window of his cell, spoke to the armed guard outside.

"What day of the month is it?" he asked.

"The fifteenth," was the answer.

The Thinking Machine made a mental astronomical calculation and satisfied himself that the moon would not rise until after nine o'clock that night. Then he asked another question. "Who attends to those courtyard lights?"

"Man from the company."

"You have no electricians in the building?"

"No."

"I should think you could save money if you had your own man."

"None of my business," replied the guard.

The guard noticed The Thinking Machine at the cell window frequently during that day, but always the face seemed listless, and there was a certain wistfulness in the squinting eyes behind the glasses. After a while he accepted the presence of the leonine head as a matter of course. He had seen other prisoners do the same thing; it was the longing for the outside world.

That afternoon, just before the day guard was relieved, the head appeared at the window again, and The Thinking Machine's hand held something out between the bars. It fluttered to the ground and the guard picked it up. It was a five-dollar bill.

"That's for you," called the prisoner.

As usual, the guard took it to the warden. That gentleman looked at it suspiciously; he looked at everything that came from Cell 13 with suspicion.

"He said it was for me," explained the guard.

"It's a sort of a tip, I suppose," said the warden. "I see no particular reason why you shouldn't accept . . ."

Suddenly he stopped. He had remembered that The Thinking Machine had gone into Cell 13 with one five-dollar bill and two ten-dollar bills; twenty-five dollars in all.

A five-dollar bill had been tied around the first pieces of linen that came from the cell. The warden still had it, and to convince himself he took it out and looked at it. It was five dollars. Yet here was another five dollars, and The Thinking Machine had only had ten-dollar bills.

"Perhaps somebody changed one of the bills for him," he thought at last, with a sigh of relief.

But then and there he made up his mind. He would search Cell 13 as a cell was never before searched in this world. When a man could write at will, and change money, and do other wholly inexplicable things, there was something radically wrong with his prison. He planned to enter the cell at night. Three o'clock would be an excellent time. The Thinking Machine must do all the weird things he did sometime. Night seemed the most reasonable.

Thus it happened that the warden stealthily descended upon Cell 13 that night at three o'clock. He paused at the door and listened. There was no sound save the steady, regular breathing of the prisoner. The keys unfastened the double locks with scarcely a clank, and the warden entered, locking the door behind him. Suddenly he flashed his light in the face of the recumbent figure.

If the warden had planned to startle The Thinking Machine, he was mistaken, for that individual merely opened his eyes quietly, reached for his glasses and inquired, in a most matter-of-fact tone, "Who is it?"

It would be useless to describe the search that the warden made. It was minute. Not one inch of the cell or the bed was overlooked. He found the round hole in the floor, and with a flash of inspiration thrust his thick fingers into it. After a moment of fumbling there he drew up something and looked at it in the light of his lantern.

"Ugh!" he exclaimed.

The thing he had taken out was a rat—a dead rat. His inspiration fled as a mist before the sun. But he continued the search. The

Thinking Machine, without a word, arose and kicked the rat out of the cell into the corridor.

The warden climbed on the bed and tried the steel bars in the tiny window. They were perfectly rigid; every bar of the door was the same.

Then the warden searched the prisoner's clothing, beginning at the shoes. Nothing hidden in them. Then the trousers waistband. Still nothing! Then the pockets of the trousers. From one side he drew out some paper money and examined it.

"Five one-dollar bills," he gasped.

"That's right," said the prisoner.

"But the . . . you had two tens and a five. What the . . . how do you do it?"

"That's my business," said the Thinking Machine.

"Did any of my men change this money for you . . . on your word of honor?"

The Thinking Machine paused just a fraction of a second.

"No," he said.

"Well, how do you do it?" asked the warden. He was prepared to believe anything.

"That's my business," again said the prisoner.

The warden glared at the eminent scientist fiercely. He felt—he knew—that this man was making a fool of him, yet he didn't know how. If he were a real prisoner, he would get the truth. But, then, perhaps, those inexplicable things which had happened would not have been brought before him so sharply. Neither of the men spoke for a long time, then suddenly the warden turned fiercely and left the cell, slamming the door behind him. He didn't dare to speak.

He glanced at the clock. It was ten minutes to four. He had hardly settled himself in bed when again came that heart-wrenching shriek through the prison. With a few muttered words he relighted his lantern and rushed through the prison again to the cell on the upper floor.

Again Ballard was crushing himself against the steel door, shrieking at the top of his voice. He stopped only when the warden flashed his lamp in the cell.

"Take me out, take me out," he screamed. "I did it. I did it. I killed her. Take it away."

"Take what away?" asked the warden.

"I threw the acid in her face. I did it. I confess. Take me out of here."

Ballard's condition was pitiable; it was only an act of mercy to let him out into the corridor. There he crouched in a corner, like an animal at bay, and clasped his hands to his ears. It took half an hour to calm him sufficiently for him to speak. Then he told incoherently what had happened. On the night before at four o'clock he had heard a voice, a sepulchral voice, muffled and wailing in tone.

"What did it say?" asked the warden, curiously.

"Acid . . . acid . . . acid!" gasped the prisoner. "It accused me. Acid! I threw the acid, and the woman died. Oh!" It was a long, shuddering wail of terror.

"Acid?" echoed the warden, puzzled. The case was beyond him.

"Acid. That's all I heard . . . that one word, repeated several times. There were other things too, but I didn't hear them."

"That was last night, eh?" asked the warden. "What happened tonight? What frightened you just now?"

"It was the same thing," gasped the prisoner. "Acid . . . acid . . . acid!" He covered his face with his hands and sat shivering. "It was acid that I used on her, but I didn't mean to kill her. I just heard the words. It was something accusing me. Accusing me." He mumbled, and was silent.

"Did you hear anything else?"

"Yes, but I couldn't understand—only a little bit—just a word or two."

"Well, what was it?"

"I heard 'acid' three times, then I heard a long, moaning sound, then . . . then . . . I heard 'Number eight hat.' I heard that twice."

"Number eight hat," repeated the warden. "What does that mean? Number eight hat? Accusing voices of conscience have never talked about size eight hats, so far as I ever heard."

"He's insane," said one of the jailers, with an air of finality.

"I believe you," said the warden. "He must be. He probably heard something and got frightened. He's trembling now. Number eight hat!"

V

When the fifth day of The Thinking Machine's imprisonment rolled around the warden was wearing a hunted look. He was anxious for the end of the thing. He could not help but feel that his distinguished prisoner had been amusing himself. And if this were so, The Thinking Machine had lost none of his sense of humor. For on this fifth day he flung down another linen note to the outside guard, bearing the words "Only two days more." Also he flung down half a dollar.

Now the warden knew—he *knew*—that the man in Cell 13 didn't have any half dollars. He couldn't have any half dollars, no more than he could have pen and ink and linen, and yet he did have them. It was a condition, not a theory; that is one reason why the warden was wearing a hunted look.

That ghastly, uncanny thing about "acid" and "number eight hat" clung to him tenaciously. They didn't mean anything, of course, merely the ravings of an insane murderer who had been driven by fear to confess his crime; still, there were so many things that "didn't mean anything" happening in the prison now since The Thinking Machine was there.

On the sixth day the warden received a letter stating that Dr. Ransome and Mr. Fielding would be at Chisholm Prison on the following evening, Thursday, and in the event Professor Van Dusen had not yet escaped—and they presumed he had not because they had not heard from him—they would meet him there.

"In case he had not yet escaped," The warden smiled grimly. Escaped!

The Thinking Machine enlivened this day for the warden with three notes. They were on the usual linen and bore generally on the appointment at half-past eight o'clock Thursday night, the very appointment the scientist had made at the time of his imprisonment.

On the afternoon of the seventh day the warden passed Cell 13 and glanced in. The Thinking Machine was lying on the iron bed, apparently sleeping lightly. The cell appeared precisely as it always did to a casual glance. The warden would swear that no man was going to leave it between that hour, it was then four o'clock, and half-past eight o'clock that evening.

On his way back past the cell the warden heard the steady breathing again, and coming close to the door looked in. He wouldn't have done so if The Thinking Machine had been looking, but now, well, it was different.

A ray of light came through the high window and fell on the face of the sleeping man. It occurred to the warden for the first time that his prisoner appeared haggard and weary. Just then The Thinking Machine stirred slightly, and the warden hurried on up the corridor guiltily. That evening after six o'clock he saw the jailer.

"Everything all right in Cell 13?" he asked.

"Yes, sir," replied the jailer. "He didn't eat much though."

It was with a feeling of having done his duty that the warden received Dr. Ransome and Mr. Fielding shortly after seven o'clock. He intended to show them the linen notes and lay before them the full story of his woes, which was a long one. But before this came to pass, the guard from the river side of the prison yard entered the office.

"The electric light in my side of the yard won't light," he informed the warden.

"That man's a jinx," thundered the official. "Everything has happened since he's been here."

The guard went back to his post in the darkness, and the warden phoned the electric light company.

"This is Chisholm Prison," he said through the phone. "Send three or four men down here quick to fix an outside light."

The reply was evidently satisfactory, for the warden hung up the receiver and went out into the yard. While Dr. Ransome and Mr. Fielding sat waiting, the guard at the outer gate came in with a special delivery letter. Dr. Ransome happened to notice the address, and when the guard went out, looked at the letter more closely.

"By George!" he exclaimed.

"What is it?" asked Mr. Fielding.

Silently the doctor offered the letter. Mr. Fielding examined it closely.

"Coincidence," he said. "It must be."

It was nearly eight o'clock when the warden returned to his office. The electricians had arrived in a wagon and were now at work. The warden pressed the buzzer communicating with the man at the outer gate in the wall.

"How many electricians came in?" he asked, over the short phone. "Four? Three workmen in jumpers and overalls and the manager? Frock coat and silk hat? All right. Be certain that only four go out. That's all."

He turned to Dr. Ransome and Mr. Fielding. "We have to be careful here . . particularly," and there was broad sarcasm in his tone, "since we have a scientist locked up."

The warden picked up the special delivery letter carelessly and then began to open it.

"When I read this I want to tell you gentlemen something about how—Great Caesar!" he ended, suddenly, as he glanced at the letter. He sat with mouth open, motionless, from astonishment.

"What is it?" asked Mr. Fielding.

"A special delivery from Cell 13," gasped the warden. "An invitation to supper."

"What?" and the two others arose, unanimously.

The warden sat dazed, staring at the letter for a moment, then called sharply to a guard outside in the corridor.

"Run down to Cell 13 and see if that man's in there."

The guard went as directed, while Dr. Ransome and Mr. Fielding examined the letter.

"It's Van Dusen's handwriting; there's no question of that," said Dr. Ransome. "I've seen too much of it."

Just then the buzz on the telephone from the outer gate sounded, and the warden, in a semitrance, picked up the receiver.

"Hello! Two reporters, eh? Let 'em come in." He turned suddenly to the doctor and Mr. Fielding. "Why, the man can't be out. He must be in his cell."

Just at that moment the guard returned.

"He's still in his cell, sir," he reported. "I saw him. He's lying down."

"There, I told you so," said the warden, and he breathed freely again. "But how did he mail that letter?"

There was a rap on the steel door which led from the jail yard into the warden's office.

"It's the reporters," said the warden. "Let them in," he instructed the guard; then to the two other gentlemen, "Don't say anything about this before them because I'd never hear the last of it."

The door opened, and the two men from the front gate entered.

"Good evening, gentlemen," said one. That was Hutchinson Hatch, the newspaper reporter. The warden knew him well.

"Well?" demanded the other irritably. "I'm here."

That was The Thinking Machine.

He squinted belligerently at the warden, who sat with mouth agape. For the moment that man had nothing to say. Dr. Ransome and Mr. Fielding were amazed, but they didn't know what the warden knew. They were only amazed; he was paralyzed. Hutchinson Hatch took in the scene with greedy eyes.

"How . . . how did you do it?" gasped the warden finally.

"Come back to the cell," said The Thinking Machine in the irritated voice which his scientific associates knew so well.

The warden, still in a condition bordering on trance, led the way.

"Flash your light in there," directed The Thinking Machine.

The warden did so. There was nothing unusual in the appearance of the cell, and there . . . there on the bed lay the figure of The Thinking Machine. Certainly! There was the yellow hair! Again the warden looked at the man beside him and wondered at the strangeness of his own dreams.

With trembling hands he unlocked the cell door and The Thinking Machine passed inside.

"See here," he said.

He kicked at the steel bars in the bottom of the cell door and three of them were pushed out of place. A fourth broke off and rolled away in the corridor.

"And here, too," directed the erstwhile prisoner as he stood on the bed to reach the small window. He swept his hand across the opening and every bar came out.

"What's this in the bed?" demanded the warden, who was beginning to recover.

"A wig," was the reply. "Turn down the cover."

The warden did so. Beneath it lay a large coil of strong rope, thirty feet or more, a dagger, three files, ten feet of electric wire, a thin, powerful pair of steel pliers, a small tack hammer with its handle, and . . . and a Derringer pistol.

"How did you do it?" demanded the warden.

"You gentlemen have an engagement to supper with me at half past nine o'clock," said The Thinking Machine. "Come on, or we shall be late."

"But how did you do it?" insisted the warden.

"Don't ever think you can stop any man who can use his brain," said The Thinking Machine. "Come on. We shall be late."

VI

It was an impatient supper party in the rooms of Professor Van Dusen—and a somewhat silent one. The guests were Dr. Ransome, Albert Fielding, the warden, and Hutchinson Hatch, reporter. The meal was served to the minute, in accordance with Professor Van Dusen's instructions of one week before. Dr. Ransome found the artichokes delicious. At last the supper was finished, and The Thinking Machine turned full on Dr. Ransome and squinted at him fiercely.

"Do you believe it now?" he demanded.

"I do," replied Dr. Ransome.

"Do you admit that it was a fair test?"

"I do."

With the others, particularly the warden, he was waiting anxiously for the explanation.

"Suppose you tell us how . . ." began Mr. Fielding.

"Yes, tell us how," said the warden.

The Thinking Machine readjusted his glasses, took a couple of preparatory squints at his audience, and began the story. He told it from the beginning logically, and no man ever talked to more interested listeners.

"My agreement was," he began, "to go into a cell, carrying nothing except what was necessary to wear, and to leave that cell within a week. I had never seen Chisholm Prison. When I went into the cell I asked for tooth powder, two ten- and one five-dollar bills, and also to have my shoes blacked. Even if these requests had been refused, it would not have mattered seriously. But you agreed to them.

"I knew there would be nothing in the cell which you thought I might use to advantage. So when the warden locked the door on me, I was apparently helpless, unless I could turn three seemingly innocent things to use. They were things which would have been permitted any prisoner under sentence of death, were they not, warden?"

"Tooth powder and polished shoes, yes, but not the money," replied the warden.

"Anything is dangerous in the hands of a man who knows how to use it," went on The Thinking Machine. "I did nothing that first night but sleep and chase rats." He glared at the warden. "When the matter was broached, I knew I could do nothing that night, so suggested the next day. You gentlemen thought I wanted time to arrange an escape with outside assistance, but this was not true. I knew I could communicate with whom I pleased, when I pleased."

The warden stared at him a moment and then settled back in his chair.

"I was aroused next morning at six o'clock by the jailer with my breakfast," continued the scientist. "He told me dinner was at twelve and supper at six. Between these times, I gathered, I would be pretty much to myself. So immediately after breakfast I examined my outside surroundings from my cell window. One look told me it would be useless to try to scale the wall, even should I decide to leave my cell by the window, for my purpose was to leave not only the cell, but the prison. Of course, I could have gone over the wall, but it would have taken me longer to lay my plans that way. Therefore, for the moment, I dismissed all idea of that.

"From this first observation I knew that the river was on that side of the prison and that there was also a playground there. Subsequently these conjectures were verified by a keeper. I knew then one important thing—that anyone might approach the prison wall from that side if necessary without attracting any particular attention. That was well to remember.

"But the outside thing which most attracted my attention was the feed wire to the electric light which ran within a few feet—

probably three or four—of my cell window. I knew that would be valuable in the event I found it necessary to cut off that light."

"Oh, you shut it off tonight, then?" asked the warden.

"Having learned all I could from that window," resumed The Thinking Machine, without heeding the interruption, "I considered the idea of escaping through the prison proper. I recalled just how I had come into the cell, which I knew would be the only way. Seven doors lay between me and the outside. So for the time being I gave up the idea of escaping that way. And I couldn't go through the solid granite walls of the cell."

The Thinking Machine paused for a moment. For several minutes there was silence and then the scientific jailbreaker went on, "While I was thinking about these things a rat ran across my foot. It suggested a new line of thought. There were at least half a dozen rats in the cell. I could see their beady eyes. Yet I had noticed none come under the cell door. I frightened them purposely and watched the cell door to see if they went out that way. They did not, but they were gone. Another way meant another opening.

"I searched for this opening and found it. It was an old drain pipe, long unused and partly choked with dirt and dust. But this was the way the rats had come. They came from somewhere. Where? Drain pipes usually lead outside prison grounds. This one probably led to the river, or near it. The rats must therefore come from that direction. If they came a part of the way, I reasoned that they came all the way because it was extremely unlikely that a solid iron or lead pipe would have any hole in it except at the exit.

"When the jailer came with my lunch, he told me two important things, although he didn't know it. One was that a new system of plumbing had been put in the prison seven years before; another that the river was only three hundred feet away. Then I knew positively that the pipe was a part of an old system. I knew, too, that it slanted generally toward the river. But did the pipe end in the water or on land?

"This was the next question to be decided. I decided it by catching several of the rats in the cell. My jailer was surprised to see me engaged in this work. I examined at least a dozen of them. They were perfectly dry; they had come through the pipe. But most important of all, they were not house rats, but field rats. The other end of the pipe was on land then, outside the prison walls. So far, so good.

"Then I knew that if I were to work freely on this point, I must attract the warden's attention in another direction. You see, by telling the warden that I had come there to escape you made the test more severe because I had to trick him by false scents."

The warden looked up with a sad expression in his eyes.

"The first thing was to make him think I was trying to communicate with you, Dr. Ransome. So I wrote a note on a piece of linen I tore from my shirt, addressed it to Dr. Ransome, tied a five dollar bill around it, and threw it out of the window. I knew the guard would take it to the warden, but I rather hoped the warden would send it as addressed. Have you that first linen note, warden?"

The warden produced the cipher.

"What does it mean anyhow?" he asked.

"Read it backward, beginning with the 'T' signature and disregard the division into words," instructed The Thinking Machine.

The warden did so.

"*T - h - i - s, this*," he spelled, studied it a moment, then read it off, grinning,

'*This is not the way I intend to escape.*' "

"Well, now what do you think o' that?" he demanded, still grinning.

"I knew that would attract your attention, just as it did," said The Thinking Machine, "and if you really found out what it was, it would be a sort of gentle rebuke."

"What did you write it with?" asked Dr. Ransome after he had examined the linen and passed it to Mr. Fielding.

"This," said the erstwhile prisoner, and he extended his foot. On it was the shoe he had worn in prison, though the polish was gone—scraped off clean. "The shoe blacking was my ink, moistened with water; the metal tip of the shoe lace made a fairly good pen."

The warden looked up and suddenly burst into a laugh, half of relief, half of amusement.

"You're a wonder," he said admiringly. "Go on."

"That precipitated a search of my cell by the warden, as I had intended," continued The Thinking Machine. "I was anxious to get the warden into the habit of searching my cell, so that eventually, constantly finding nothing, he would get disgusted and quit. This happened at last."

The warden blushed.

"He then took my white shirt away and gave me a prison shirt. He was satisfied that those two pieces of the shirt were all that was missing. But while he was searching my cell I had another piece of that same shirt, about nine inches square, rolled into a small ball in my mouth."

"Nine inches off that shirt?" demanded the warden." Where did it come from?"

"The fronts of all stiff white shirts are of triple thickness," was the explanation. "I tore out one thickness, leaving only two thicknesses. I knew you wouldn't see it. So much for that."

There was a little pause, and the warden looked from one to another of the men with a sheepish grin.

"Having disposed of the warden for the time being by giving him something else to think about, I took my first real step toward freedom," said Professor Van Dusen. "I knew within reason that the pipe led somewhere to the playground outside; I knew a great many boys played there; I knew that rats came into my cell from out there. Could I communicate with some one outside with these things at hand?

"First was necessary, I saw, a long and fairly reliable thread, so . . . but here," he pulled up his trousers legs and showed that the tops of both stockings, of fine, strong lisle, were gone. "I unraveled those—after I got them started it wasn't difficult—and I had easily a quarter of a mile of thread that I could depend on.

"Then on half of my remaining linen I wrote, laboriously enough I assure you, a letter explaining my situation to this gentleman here," and he indicated Hutchinson Hatch. "I knew he would assist me for the value of the newspaper story. I tied firmly to this linen letter a ten-dollar bill—there is no surer way of attracting the eye of anyone—and wrote on the linen: 'Finder of this, deliver to Hutchinson Hatch, *Daily American*, who will give another ten dollars for the information.'

"The next thing was to get this note outside on that playground where a boy might find it. There were two ways, but I chose the best. I took one of the rats—I became adept in catching them—tied the linen and money firmly to one leg, fastened my lisle thread to another, and turned him loose in the drain pipe. I reasoned that the natural fright of the rodent would make him run until he was outside the pipe and then out on earth he would probably stop to gnaw off the linen and money.

"From the moment the rat disappeared into that dusty pipe, I became anxious. I was taking so many chances. The rat might gnaw the string, of which I held one end; other rats might gnaw it; the rat might run out of the pipe and leave the linen and money where they would never be found; a thousand other things might have happened. So began some nervous hours, but the fact that the rat ran on until only a few feet of the string remained in my cell made me think he was outside the pipe. I had carefully instructed Mr. Hatch what to do in case the note reached him. The question was: Would it reach him?

"This done, I could only wait and make other plans in case this one failed. I openly attempted to bribe my jailer, and learned from him that he held the keys to only two of seven doors between me and freedom. Then I did something else to make the warden nervous. I took the steel supports out of the heels of my shoes and made a pretense of sawing the bars of my cell window. The warden raised a pretty row about that. He developed, too, the habit of shaking the bars of my cell window to see if they were solid. They were—then."

Again the warden grinned. He had ceased being astonished.

"With this one plan I had done all I could and could only wait to see what happened," the scientist went on." I couldn't know whether my note had been delivered or even found, or whether the rat had gnawed it up. And I didn't dare to draw back through the pipe that one slender thread which connected me with the outside.

"When I went to bed that night I didn't sleep for fear there would come the slight signal twitch at the thread which was to tell me that Mr. Hatch had received the note. At half-past three o'clock, I judge, I felt this twitch, and no prisoner actually under sentence of death ever welcomed a thing more heartily."

The Thinking Machine stopped and turned to the reporter.

"You'd better explain just what you did," he said.

"The linen note was brought to me by a small boy who had been playing baseball," said Mr. Hatch. "I immediately saw a big story in it, so I gave the boy another ten dollars and got several spools of silk, some twine, and a roll of light, pliable wire. The professor's note suggested that I have the finder of the note show me just where it was picked up, and told me to make my search from there, beginning at two o'clock in the morning. If I found the other end of the thread I was to twitch it gently three times, then a fourth.

"I began the search with a small flashlight. It was an hour and twenty minutes before I found the end of the drain pipe, half hidden in weeds. The pipe was very large there, say twelve inches across. Then I found the end of the thread, twitched it as directed and immediately I got an answering twitch.

"Then I fastened the silk to this and Professor Van Dusen began to pull it into his cell. I nearly had heart disease for fear the string would break. To the end of the silk I fastened the twine, and when that had been pulled in, I tied on the wire. Then that was drawn into the pipe, and we had a substantial line, which rats couldn't gnaw, from the mouth of the drain into the cell."

The Thinking Machine raised his hand, and Hatch stopped.

"All this was done in absolute silence," said the scientist. "But when the wire reached my hand I could have shouted. Then we tried another experiment, which Mr. Hatch was prepared for. I tested the pipe as a speaking tube. Neither of us could hear very clearly, but I dared not speak loud for fear of attracting attention in the prison. At last I made him understand what I wanted immediately. He seemed to have great difficulty in understanding when I asked for nitric acid, and I repeated the word 'acid' several times.

"Then I heard a shriek from a cell above me. I knew instantly that some one had overheard, and when I heard you coming, Mr. Warden, I feigned sleep. If you had entered my cell at that moment that whole plan of escape would have ended there. But you passed on. That was the nearest I ever came to being caught.

"Having established this improvised trolley it is easy to see how I got things in the cell and made them disappear at will. I merely dropped them back into the pipe. You, Mr. Warden, could not have reached the connecting wire with your hand; it is too large. My hand, you see, is longer and my fingers more slender. In addition I guarded the top of that pipe with a rat. You remember how."

"I remember," said the warden with a grimace.

"I thought that if any one were tempted to investigate that hole, the rat would dampen his ardor. Mr. Hatch could not send me anything useful through the pipe until next night although he did send me change for ten dollars as a test, so I proceeded with other parts of my plan. Then I evolved the method of escape, which I finally employed.

"In order to carry this out successfully, it was necessary for the guard in the yard to get accustomed to seeing me at the cell window. I arranged this by dropping linen notes to him, boastful in tone, to make the warden believe, if possible, that one of his assistants was communicating with the outside for me. I would stand at my window for hours gazing out, so the guard could see, and occasionally I spoke to him. In that way I learned that the prison had no electricians of its own but was dependent upon the lighting company should anything go wrong.

"That cleared the way to freedom perfectly. Early in the evening of the last day of my imprisonment, when it was dark, I planned to cut the feed wire which was only a few feet from my window, reaching it with an acid-tipped wire I had. That would make that side of the prison perfectly dark while the electricians were searching for the break. That would also bring Mr. Hatch into the prison yard.

"There was only one more thing to do before I actually began the work of setting myself free. This was to arrange final details with Mr. Hatch through our speaking tube. I did this within half an hour after the warden left my cell on the fourth night of my imprisonment. Mr. Hatch again had serious difficulty in understanding me, and I repeated the word 'acid' to him several times, and later the words 'number eight hat'—that's my size—and these were the things which made a prisoner upstairs confess to murder, so one of the jailers told me next day. This prisoner heard our voices, confused of course, through the pipe, which also went to his cell. The cell directly over me was not occupied, hence no one else heard.

"Of course the actual work of cutting the steel bars out of the window and door was comparatively easy with nitric acid, which I got through the pipe in thin bottles, but it took time. Hour after hour on the fifth and sixth and seven days the guard below was looking at me as I worked on the bars of the window with the acid on a piece of wire. I used the tooth powder to prevent the acid spreading. I looked away abstractedly as I worked and each minute the acid cut deeper into the metal. I noticed that the jailers always tried the door by shaking the upper part, never the lower bars, therefore I cut the lower bars, leaving them hanging in place by thin strips of metal. But that was a bit of daredevilry. I could not have gone that way so easily."

The Thinking Machine sat silent for several minutes.

"I think that makes everything clear," he went on. "Whatever points I have not explained were merely to confuse the warden and jailers. These items found in my bed I simply brought in to please Mr. Hatch, who wanted to improve the story. Of course, the wig was necessary in my plan. The special delivery letter I wrote in my cell with Mr. Hatch's fountain pen. I sent it out to him, and he mailed it. That's all, I think."

"But your actually leaving the prison grounds and then coming in through the outer gate to my office?" asked the warden.

"Perfectly simple," said the scientist. "I cut the electric light wire with acid, as I said, when the current was off. Therefore when the current was turned on, the yard light didn't light. I knew it would take some time to find out what was the matter and make repairs. When the guard went to report to you the yard was dark. I crept out the window—it was a tight fit, too—and replaced the bars while standing on a narrow ledge and remained in a shadow until the force of electricians arrived. Mr. Hatch was one of them.

"When I saw him, I spoke, and he handed me a cap, a jumper, and overalls, which I put on within ten feet of you, Mr. Warden, while you were in the yard. Later Mr. Hatch called me, presumably as a workman, and together we went out the gate to get something out of the wagon. The gate guard let us pass out readily as two workmen who had just passed in. We changed our clothing and reappeared, asking to see you. We saw you. That's all."

There was silence for several minutes. Dr. Ransome was first to speak.

"Wonderful!" he exclaimed. "Perfectly amazing."

"How did Mr. Hatch happen to come with the electricians?" asked Mr. Fielding.

"His father is manager of the company," replied The Thinking Machine.

"But what if there had been no Mr. Hatch outside to help?"

"Every prisoner has one friend outside who would help him escape if he could."

"Suppose—just suppose—that there had been no old plumbing system there?" asked the warden, curiously.

"There were two other ways out," said The Thinking Machine, enigmatically.

Ten minutes later the telephone rang. It was a request for the warden.

"Light all right, eh?" the warden asked through the phone. "Good. Wire cut beside Cell 13? Yes, I know. One electrician too many? What's that? Two came out?"

The warden turned to the others with a puzzled expression.

"He only let in four electricians, he has let out two and says there are three left."

"Right. I was the odd one," said The Thinking Machine.

"Oh," said the warden. "I see." Then through the phone, "Let the fifth man go. He's all right."

3

THE PROBLEM OF THE BROKEN BRACELET

The girl in the green mask leaned against the foot of the bed and idly fingered a revolver which lay in the palm of her daintily gloved hand. The dim glow of the night lamp enveloped her softly and added a sinister glint to the bright steel of the weapon. Cowering in the bed was another figure—the figure of a woman. Sheets and blankets were drawn up tightly to her chin, and her startled eyes peered anxiously, as if fascinated, at the revolver.

"Now please don't scream," warned the masked girl. Her voice was quite casual, the tone in which one might have discussed an affair of far removed personal interest. "It would be perfectly useless, and dangerous besides."

"Who are you?" gasped the woman in the bed, staring horror stricken at the inscrutable mask of her visitor. "What do you want?"

A faint flicker of amusement lay in the shadowy eyes of the masked girl, and her red lips twitched slightly. "I don't think I can be mistaken," she said and then inquired, "You are Miss Isabel Leigh Harding?"

"Y-yes," was the chattering reply.

"Originally of Virginia?"

"Yes."

"Great-granddaughter of William Tremaine Harding, an officer in the Continental Army about 1775?"

The inflection of the questioning voice had risen almost imperceptibly, but the tone remained cold and exquisitely courteous. At the last question the masked girl leaned forward a little expectantly.

"Yes," faltered Miss Harding faintly.

"Good, very good," commented the masked girl, and there was a note of repressed triumph in her voice. "I congratulate you, Miss Harding, upon your self-control. Under the same circumstances most women would have begun by screaming. I would have myself."

"But who are you?" demanded Miss Harding again. "How did you get in here? What do you want?"

She sat bolt upright in bed with less fear now than curiosity in her manner, and her luxuriant hair tumbled about her shoulders in profuse dishevelment.

At the sudden movement the masked girl took a firmer grip on the revolver and moved it forward a little threateningly. "Now please, don't make any mistake!" she advised Miss Harding pleasantly. "You will notice that I have drawn the bell rope up beyond your reach and knotted it. The servants are on the floor above in the extreme rear, and I doubt if they would hear you scream. Your companion is away for the night, and then there is this." She tapped her weapon significantly. "Furthermore, you will notice that the lamp is beyond your reach, and you cannot extinguish it as long as you remain in bed."

Miss Harding saw all these things and was convinced.

"Now as to your question," continued the masked girl quietly. "My identity is of absolutely no concern or importance to you. You would not even recognize my name if I gave it to you. How did I get here? By opening an unfastened window in the drawing room on the first floor and walking in. I shall leave it unlatched when I go; so perhaps you had better have someone fasten it; otherwise

45

thieves may enter." She smiled a little at the astonishment in Miss Harding's face. "Now as to why I am here and what I want."

She sat down on the foot of the bed and drew her cloak more closely about her, and folded her hands in her lap. Miss Harding placed a pillow and lounged against it comfortably, watching her visitor in astonishment. Except for the mask and the revolver, it might have been a cozy chat in any woman's boudoir.

"I came here to borrow from you—*borrow*, understand," the masked girl went on, "the least valuable article in your jewel box."

"My jewel box!" gasped Miss Harding suddenly. She had just thought of it and glanced around at the table where it lay open.

"Don't alarm yourself," the masked girl remarked reassuringly, "I have removed nothing from it."

The light of the lamp fell full upon the open casket where radiated multicolored flashes of gems. Miss Harding craned her neck a little to see, and seeing sank back against her pillow with a sigh of relief.

"As I said, I came to borrow one thing," the masked girl continued evenly. "If I cannot borrow it, I shall take it."

Miss Harding sat for a moment in mute contemplation of her visitor. She was searching her mind for some tangible explanation of this nightmarish thing. After awhile she shook her head, meaning that even guesswork was futile. "What particular article do you want?" she asked finally.

"Specifically, according to a letter from the prison in which he was executed by order of the British commander, your great-grandfather, William Tremaine Harding, left to your grandfather a gold bracelet, a plain band," the masked girl explained. "Your grandfather received the bracelet when he turned twenty-one years old, from the persons who held it in trust for him, and on his death, March 25, 1853, he left it to your father. Your father died intestate in April, 1898, and the bracelet passed into your mother's keeping, there being no son. Your mother died within the last year. Therefore, the bracelet is now, or should be, in your possession. You see," she concluded, "I have taken pains to acquaint myself with your family history."

"You have," Miss Harding assented. "And may I ask why you want this bracelet?"

"And I answer that it is no concern of yours."

"You said *borrow* it, I believe?"

"Either I will borrow it or take it."

"Is there any certainty that it will ever be returned? And if so, when?"

"You will have to take my word for that, of course," replied the masked girl. "I shall return it within a few days."

Miss Harding glanced at her jewel box. "Have you looked there?" she inquired.

"Yes," replied the masked girl. "It isn't there."

"Not there?" repeated Miss Harding.

"If it had been there, I would have taken it and gone away without disturbing you," the masked girl went on. "Its absence is what caused me to wake you."

"Not there," said Miss Harding again wonderingly, and she moved as if to get up.

"Don't do that, please," warned the masked girl quickly. "I shall hand you the box if you like."

She arose and passed the casket to Miss Harding, who spilled out the contents in her lap.

"Why, it is gone!" she exclaimed.

"Yes, from there," said the other a little grimly. "Now please tell me immediately where it is. It will save trouble."

"I don't know," replied Miss Harding hopelessly.

The masked girl stared at her coldly for a moment and then drew back the hammer of the revolver until it clicked.

Miss Harding stared in sudden terror.

"All this is merely time wasted," said the masked girl sternly, coldly. "Either the bracelet or this!" Again she tapped the revolver.

"If it is not here, I don't know where it is," Miss Harding rushed on desperately. "I placed it here at ten o'clock tonight—here in this box—when I undressed. I don't know—I can't imagine . . ."

The masked girl tapped the revolver again several times with one gloved finger. "The bracelet," she demanded impatiently.

Fear was in Miss Harding's eyes now, and she made a helpless, pleading gesture with both white hands. "You wouldn't kill me—murder me!" she gasped. "I don't know. Here, take the other jewels. I can't tell you."

"The other jewels are of absolutely no use to me," said the girl coldly. "I want only the bracelet."

"On my honor," faltered Miss Harding, "I don't know where it is. I can't imagine what has happened to it. I—I—" she stopped helplessly.

The masked girl raised the weapon threateningly, and Miss Harding stared in cringing horror.

"Please, please, I don't know!" she pleaded hysterically.

For a little while the masked girl was thoughtfully silent. One shoe tapped the floor rhythmically; the eyes were contracted. "I believe you," she said slowly at last. She arose suddenly and drew her coat closely about her. "Good night," she added as she started toward the door. There she turned back. "It would not be wise for you to give an alarm for at least half an hour. Then you had better have someone latch the window in the drawing room. I shall leave it unfastened. Good night."

And she was gone.

Hutchinson Hatch, reporter, had finished relating the story to The Thinking Machine, incident by incident, just as it had been reported to Chief of Detectives Mallory, when the eminent scientist's aged servant, Martha, tapped on the door of the reception room and entered with a card.

"A lady to see you, sir," she announced.

The scientist extended one slender white hand, took the card, and glanced at it.

"Your story is merely what Miss Harding told the police?" he inquired of the reporter. "You didn't get it from Miss Harding herself?"

"No, I didn't see her."

"Show the lady in, Martha," directed The Thinking Machine. She turned and went out, and he passed the card to the reporter.

"By George! It's Miss Harding herself!" Hatch exclaimed. "Now we can get it all straight."

There was a little pause, and Martha ushered a young woman into the room. She was girlish, slender, daintily yet immaculately attired, with deep brown eyes, firmly molded chin and mouth, and wavy hair. Hatch's expression of curiosity gave way to one of frank admiration as he regarded her. There was only the most impersonal sort of interest in the watery blue eyes of The Thinking Machine. She stood for a moment with gaze alternating between the distinguished man of science and the reporter.

"I am Mr. Van Dusen," explained The Thinking Machine. "Allow me, Miss Harding—Mr. Hatch."

The girl smiled and offered a gloved hand cordially to each of the two men. The Thinking Machine merely touched it respectfully; Hatch shook it warmly.

"Be seated, Miss Harding," the scientist invited.

"I hardly know just what I came to say and just how to say it," she began uncertainly and smiled a little. "And anyway I had hoped that you were alone, so . . ."

"You may speak with perfect freedom before Mr. Hatch," interrupted The Thinking Machine. "Perhaps I shall be able to aid you, but first will you repeat the history of the bracelet as nearly as you can in the words of the masked woman who called upon you so . . . so unconventionally?"

The girl's brows were lifted inquiringly with a sort of start.

"We were discussing the case when your card was brought in," continued The Thinking Machine tersely. "We shall continue from that point if you will be so good."

The young woman recited the history of the bracelet, slowly and carefully.

"And that statement of the case is correct?" questioned the scientist.

"Absolutely, so far as I know," was the reply.

"And as I understand it, you were in the house alone; that is, alone except for the servants?"

"Yes; I live there alone, except for a boarder and two servants. The servants were not within the sound of my voice even if I had screamed, and Miss Talbott, my boarder, was out for the night."

The Thinking Machine had dropped back into his chair, with squinting eyes turned upward and long white fingers pressed tip to tip. He sat thus silently for a long time. The girl at last broke the silence.

"Naturally I am a little surprised," she remarked falteringly, "that I should have appeared here just in time to interrupt a discussion of the odd occurrence in my home last night, but really—"

"This bracelet," interrupted the little scientist again. "It was of oval form, perhaps, with no stones set in it, or anything of that sort—merely a band that fastened with an invisible hinge. That's right, I believe?"

"Quite right, yes," replied the girl readily.

It occurred to Hatch suddenly that he himself did not know—in fact, had not inquired—the shape of the bracelet. He knew only that it was gold and of no great value. Knowing nothing about what it looked like, he had not described it to The Thinking Machine; therefore he raised his eyes inquiringly now. The drawn face of the scientist was inscrutable.

"As I started to say," the girl went on, "the bracelet and the events of last night have no direct connection with the purpose of my visit here."

"Indeed?" commented the scientist.

"No, I came to see if you could assist me in another way. For instance," and she fumbled in her pocketbook, "I happened to know, Professor Van Dusen, of some of the remarkable things you have accomplished, and I should like to ask if you can throw any light on this for me."

She drew from the pocketbook a crumpled, yellow sheet of paper—a strip perhaps an inch wide, thin as tissue, glazed, and extraordinarily wrinkled. The Thinking Machine squinted at its manifold irregularities for an instant curiously, nodded, sniffed at it and then slowly began to unfold it, smoothing it out carefully as he went. Hatch leaned forward eagerly and stared. He was more than a little astonished at the end to find that the sheet was blank. The Thinking Machine examined both sides of the paper thoughtfully.

"And where did you find the bracelet at last?" he inquired casually.

"I have reason to believe," the girl rushed on suddenly, disregarding the question, "that this strip of paper has been substituted for one of real value, perhaps of great value. I don't know how to proceed unless—"

"Where did you find the bracelet?" demanded The Thinking Machine again impatiently.

Hatch would have hesitated a long time before he would have said the girl was disconcerted at the question, or that there had been any real change in the expression of her pretty face.

"After the masked woman had gone," she went on calmly, "I summoned the servants, and we made a search. We found the bracelet at last. I thought I had tossed it into my jewel box when I removed it last night, but it seems I was careless enough to let it fall down behind my dressing table, and it was there all the time the . . . the masked woman was in my room."

"And when did you make this discovery?" asked The Thinking Machine.

"Within a few minutes after she went out."

"In making your search, you were guided perhaps by a belief that in the natural course of events the bracelet could not have disappeared from your jewel box unless someone had entered the room before the masked woman entered; and further that if anyone had entered, you would have been awakened?"

"Precisely." There was another pause. "And now please," she went on, "what does this blank strip of paper mean?"

"You had expected something with writing on it, of course?"

"That's just what I had expected," and she laughed nervously. "You may rest assured I was considerably surprised at finding that."

"I can imagine you were," remarked the scientist dryly.

The conversation had reached a point where Hatch was hopelessly lost. The young woman and the scientist were talking with mutual understanding of things that seemed to have no connection with anything that had gone before. What was the paper anyway? Where did it come from? What connection did it have with the affairs of the previous night? How did—

"Mr. Hatch, a match, please," requested The Thinking Machine.

Wonderingly the reporter produced one and handed it over. The imperturbable man of science lighted it and thrust the mysterious paper into the blaze. The girl arose with a sudden, startled cry and snatched at the paper desperately, extinguishing the match as she did so. The Thinking Machine turned disapproving eyes on her.

"I thought you were going to burn it!" she gasped.

"There is not the slightest danger of that, Miss Harding," declared The Thinking Machine coldly. He examined the blank sheet again. "This way, please."

He arose and led the way into his tiny laboratory across the narrow hall, with the girl following. Hatch trailed behind, wondering vaguely what it was all about. A small burner flashed into flame as The Thinking Machine applied a match, and curious eyes peered over his shoulders as he held the blank strip, now smoothed out, so that the rising heat would strike it.

For a long time three pairs of eyes were fastened on the mysterious paper, all with understanding now, but nothing appeared. Hatch glanced around at the young woman. Her face wore an expression of tense excitement. The red lips were slightly parted in anticipation, the eyes sparkling, and the cheeks flushed deeply.

Then suddenly the exclamation burst from her triumphantly, "There! There! Do you see?"

Faint, scrawly lines grew on the strip suspended over the flame. Totally oblivious of their presence apparently, The Thinking Machine was squinting steadily at the paper. It was slowly crinkling up into wavy lines under the influence of the heat. Gradually the edges were charring, and the odor of scorched paper filled the room. Still the scientist held the paper over the fire. Just as it seemed inevitable that it would burst into flame, he withdrew it and turned to the girl.

"There was no substitution," he remarked tersely. "It is invisible ink."

"What does it say?" demanded the young woman abruptly. "What does it mean?"

The Thinking Machine spread the scorched strip of paper on the table before them carefully at length studied it minutely.

"Really, my dear young woman, I don't know," he said crabbedly at last. "It may take days to find out what it means."

"But something's written there! Read it!" the girl insisted.

"Read it for yourself," said the scientist impatiently. "No, don't touch it. It will crumble to pieces."

Faintly, yet decipherable under a magnifying glass, the three were able to make out this on the paper:

> Stonehedge—idim-sérpa'l ed serueh siort tnaeG ed
> etéT al rap eétej erbmo'l ed tniop ud zerit sruO'd rehcoR
> ud eueuq ud dron ua sdeip tnec. W.F.H.

"What does it mean? What does it mean?" demanded the young woman impatiently. "What does it mean?"

The sudden hardening of her tone caused both Hatch and The Thinking Machine to turn and stare at her. Some strange change had come over her face. There was chagrin, perhaps, and there was more than that—a merciless glitter in the brown eyes, a grim expression about the chin and mouth, a greedy closing and unclosing of the small, well-shaped hands.

"I presume it's a cipher of some sort," remarked The Thinking Machine curtly. "It may take time to read it and to learn definitely just where the treasure is hidden, and you may have to wait for—"

"Treasure!" exclaimed the girl. "Did you say treasure? There is treasure then?"

The Thinking Machine shrugged his shoulders. "What else?" he asked. "Now, please, let me see the bracelet."

"The bracelet!" the girl repeated, and again Hatch noted that quick change of expression on the pretty face. "I . . . er . . . must you see it? I . . . er . . ." And she stopped.

"It is absolutely necessary, if I make anything of this," and the scientist indicated the charred paper. "You have it in your pocketbook, of course."

The girl stepped forward suddenly and leaned over the laboratory table, intently studying the mysterious strip of paper. At last she raised her head as if she had reached a decision.

"I have only a part of the bracelet," she announced, "only half. It was unavoidably broken, and—"

"Only half?" interrupted The Thinking Machine, and he squinted coldly into the young woman's eyes.

"Here it is," she said at last, desperately almost. "I don't know where the other half is. It would be useless to ask me."

She drew an aged, badly scratched half circlet of gold from her pocketbook, handed it to the scientist and then went and looked out the window. He examined it—the delicate decorative tracings, then the invisible hinge where the bracelet had been rudely torn apart. Twice he raised his squinting eyes and stared at the girl as she stood silhouetted against the light of the window. When he spoke again, there was a deeper note in his voice, a singular softening, an unusual deference.

"I shall read the cipher of course, Miss Harding," he said slowly. "It may take an hour, or it may take a week, I don't know." Again he scrutinized the charred paper. "Do you speak French?" he inquired suddenly.

"Enough to understand and to make myself understood," said the girl. "Why?"

The Thinking Machine scribbled off a copy of the cipher and handed it to her.

"I'll communicate with you when I reach a conclusion," he remarked. "Please leave your address on your card here," and he handed her the card and pencil.

"You know my home address," she said. "Perhaps it would be better for me to call this afternoon late or tomorrow."

"I'd prefer to have your address," said the scientist. "As I say, I don't know when I shall be able to speak definitely."

The girl paused for a moment and tapped the blunt end of the pencil against her white teeth thoughtfully with her left hand. "As a matter of fact," she said at last, "I am not returning home now. The events of last night have shaken me considerably, and I am now on my way to Blank Rock, a little seashore town where I shall remain for a few days. My address there will be the High Tower."

"Write it down, please!" directed The Thinking Machine tersely. The girl stared at him strangely with a challenge in her eyes and then she leaned over the table to write. Before the pencil had touched the card, however, she changed her mind and handed both to Hatch with a smile.

"Please write it for me," she requested. "I write a wretched hand anyway, and besides I have on my gloves." She turned again to the little scientist, who stood squinting over her head. "Thank you so much for your trouble," she said in conclusion. "You can reach me at this address either by wire or letter for the next fortnight."

And a few minutes later she was gone. For awhile The Thinking Machine was silent as he again studied the faint writing on the strip of paper.

"The cipher," he remarked to Hatch at last, "is no cipher at all; it's so simple. But there are some other things I shall have to find out first, and . . . suppose you drop by early tomorrow to see me."

Half an hour later The Thinking Machine went to the telephone, and after running through the book called a number.

"Is Miss Harding home yet?" he demanded, when an answer came.

"No, sir," was the reply, in a woman's voice.

"Would you mind telling me, please, if she is left handed?"

"Why, no, sir. She's right handed. Who is this?"

"I knew it, of course. Good bye."

The Thinking Machine was squinting into the inquiring eyes of Hutchinson Hatch.

"The reason that the police are so frequently unsuccessful in explaining the mysteries of crime," he remarked, "is not through lack of natural intelligence or through lack of a birth-given aptitude for the work, but rather through the lack of an absolutely accurate knowledge which is wide enough to enable them to proceed. Now here is a case in point. It starts with a cipher, goes into an intricate astronomical calculation, and from that into simple geometry. The difficulty with the detectives is not that they could not work out each of these as it was presented, perhaps with the aid of some out-sider, but that they would not recognize the existence of the three phases of the problem in the first place.

"You have heard me say frequently, Mr. Hatch, that logic is inevitable—as inevitable as that two and two make four not some-times, but all the time. That is true, but it must have an indisputable starting point—the one unit which is unassailable. In this case unit produces unit in order, and the proper array of these units gives a coherent answer. Let me demonstrate briefly just what I mean.

"A masked woman, employing at least the method of a thief, demands a certain bracelet of this Miss . . . Miss Harding. (Is that her name?) She doesn't want jewels; she wants that bracelet. Whatever other conjectures may be advanced, the one dominant fact is that this one bracelet, itself of little comparative value, is worth more than all the rest to her—the masked woman, I mean—and she has endangered liberty and perhaps life to get it. Why? The history of the bracelet as she herself stated it to Miss Harding gives the answer. A man in prison, under sentence of death, had that bracelet at one time. We can conjecture immediately, therefore, that the masked woman knew that the fact of its having been in this man's possession gave him an opportunity at least of so marking the bracelet, or of confiding in it a valuable secret. One's first thought, therefore, is of treasure . . . hidden treasure. We shall go further and suggest treasure hidden by a Continental officer to prevent its falling into other hands. This officer under sentence of death, and therefore cut off from all communication with the outside, took a desperate means of communicating the location of the treasure to his heirs. That is clear, isn't it?"

The reporter nodded.

"I described the bracelet—you heard me—and yet I had never seen it, nor had I a description of it. That description was merely a preliminary test of the truth of the first assumptions. I reasoned that the bracelet must be of a type which could be employed to carry a message safely past prying eyes; and there is really only one sort which is feasible, and that is the one I described. These bracelets are always hollow; the invisible hinges hold them together on one side, and they lock on the other. It would be perfectly possible, therefore, to write the message the prisoner wanted to send out on a strip of paper and cram it into the bracelet at the lock end. In that event it would certainly pass minute inspection; the only difficulty would be for the outside person to find it.

"When the young woman came here and produced a strip of thin paper, apparently blank, with the multitude of wrinkles in it, I immediately saw that that paper had been recovered from the brace-let. It was old, yellow, and worn. Therefore, blank or not, that was the message which the prisoner had sent out. You saw me hold it over the flame and saw the characters appear. It was invisible ink, of course.

"Hard to make in prison, you say? Not at all. Writing either with lemon juice or milk, once dry, is perfectly invisible on paper; but when exposed to heat at any time afterward, it will appear. That is a chemical truth.

"Now the thing that appeared was a cipher—an absurd one, still a cipher. Extraordinary precaution of the prisoner who was about to die! This cipher—let me see exactly," and the scientist spelled it out:

> *"Stonehedge—idim-sérpa'l ed serueh siort tnaeG ed etéT al rap eétej erbmo'l ed tniop ud zerit sruO'd rehcoR ud eueuq ud dron ua sdeip tnec."*

"If you know anything of languages, Mr. Hatch," he contin-ued, "you know that French is the only language where the apostro-phe and the accent marks play a very important part. A moment's study of this particular cipher therefore convinced me that it was in French. I tried the simple expedient of reading it backward, with this result:

> *"Stonehedge. Cent pieds au nord du queue du Rocher d'Ours tirez du point de l'ombre jetée par La Téte de Geant trois heures de l'aprés-midi."*

"Here, therefore, was a sensible statement in French, which translated freely into English is simply:

> *"Stonehedge. Hundred feet due north from tail of Bear Rock through apex (or point) of shadow cast by Giant's Head, three p.m."*

"I had read the cipher and knew its English translation before I gave a copy of it to the young woman who was here. I specifically asked her if she knew French, to give her a clue by which she might interpret the cipher herself. And thus I blazed the way within a few minutes to the point where astronomical and geometrical calculations were next. Please bear in mind that this message from the dead was not dated.

"Now, about the young woman herself," continued the scientist after a moment. "The statement of how she came to find the bracelet was obviously untrue; particularly are we convinced of this when she cannot, or will not, explain how it was broken. Therefore, another field is open for scrutiny. The bracelet was broken. If we assume that it is the bracelet, and there is no reason to doubt it, and we know it is in her possession, we know also that more than one person had been searching for it. We know positively that that other person—not the masked girl, but the one who had preceded her to Miss Harding's room on the same night—got the bracelet from Miss Harding, and we are safe in assuming that it passed out of that other person's hand by force. The bracelet had been literally torn apart at the hinge. In other words, there must have been a physical contest, and one piece of the circlet—the piece with the message—passed out of the hands of the person who had preceded the masked woman and stolen the bracelet.

"But this is by the way. Stonehedge is the name of the old Tremaine Harding estate, about twenty miles out, and there all of the Harding family valuables were hidden by William Tremaine Harding, who died by bullet, a martyr to the cause of freedom. We shall get the treasure this afternoon after I have settled one or two dates and made the astronomical and geometrical calculations which are necessary."

There was silence for a minute or more, broken at last by the impatient *honk, honk!* of an automobile outside.

"We'll go now," announced The Thinking Machine as he arose. "There is a car for us."

He led the way out, Hatch following. A heavy touring car, with three seats, driven by a young woman, was waiting at the door. The woman was a stranger to the reporter, but there was no introduction.

"Did you get the date of Captain Harding's imprisonment?" asked The Thinking Machine.

"Yes," was the reply, "June 3, 1776."

The Thinking Machine clambered in, Hatch following silently, and the car rushed away. It paused in a suburb long enough to pick up two workmen with picks and shovels, who took their places in the back seat, and then the automobile with its strange company—a pretty woman, a newspaper reporter, a distinguished scientist, and two laborers—proceeded on its way. Hatch, alone in the second seat, heard only one remark by the scientist, which was this:

"Of course, she was clever enough to read the cipher after I gave her the hint that it was in French, so we shall find that the place has been dug over; but there is only one chance in three hundred and sixty-five that the treasure was found. I give her credit for extraordinary cleverness, but not enough to make the necessary astronomical calculations."

A drive of an hour and a half brought them to Stonehedge, a huge old estate with a ramshackle dwelling and acres of rock-ridden ground. Away off in the northwest corner were two large stones, Bear Rock and Giant's Head, rising fifteen or twenty feet above the ground. The car was driven over a rough road and stopped near them.

"You see, she did read the cipher," remarked the scientist placidly. "Workmen have already been here."

Straight ahead of them was an excavation ten feet or more square. Hatch peered into it, while The Thinking Machine busied himself by planting a stake at the so-called tail of Bear Rock. Then he glanced at his watch. It was half past two o'clock. He sat down with the young woman in the shadow of Giant's Head. Hatch lounged on the ground near them, and the workmen made themselves comfortable in their own way.

"We can't do anything till three o'clock," remarked The Thinking Machine.

"And just what shall we do then?" inquired the young woman expectantly. It was the first time she had spoken since they started.

"It is rather difficult to explain," said The Thinking Machine. "The hole there proves that the young woman read the cipher, of course. Now here briefly is why the treasure was not found. Today is September 17. A measurement was made according to instructions from the tail of Bear Rock through the apex of the shadow of Giant's Head precisely at three o'clock yesterday, one hundred feet due north, or as near north as possible. The hole shows the end of the hundred-foot line. Now, we know that Captain Harding was imprisoned on June 3, 1776; we know he buried the treasure before that date; we have a right to assume that it was only shortly before. On June 3 of any year the apex of the shadow will be in a totally different place from September 17, because of the movement of the earth about the sun and the relative changes in the sun's position. What we must do now is to find precisely where the shadow falls at three o'clock today, then make our calculations to show where it will fall say one week before June 3. Do you follow me? In other words, a difference of half a foot in the location of the apex of the shadow will make a difference of many feet at the end of one hundred feet when we follow the cipher."

At precisely three o'clock The Thinking Machine noted the position of the shadow, and then began a calculation which covered two sheets of blank paper which Hatch had in his pocket.

"This is correct," said The Thinking Machine at last. He arose and planted another stake in the ground. "There is a chance, of course, that we misfire the first time because of possible seismic disturbances at sometime past or of a change in the surface of the ground, but this is mathematically correct."

Then, with the assistance of the newspaperman and the young woman, he drew his hundred-foot line and planted a third stake.

"Dig here," he told the workmen.

One hour later the long lost family plate and jewels of the ancient Harding family had been unearthed. The Thinking Machine and the others stooped over the rotting box which had been brought to the surface and noted the contents. Roughly, the value was above two hundred thousand dollars.

"And I think that is all, Miss Harding," said the scientist at last. "It is yours. Load it into your car there and drive home."

"Miss Harding!" Hatch repeated quickly, with a glance at the young woman. "Miss Harding?"

The Thinking Machine turned and squinted at the reporter for a moment. "Didn't you know that the young woman who called on me was not Miss Harding?" he demanded. "It was evident in her every act, in her failing to explain the broken bracelet and in the fact that she was left handed. You must have noticed that. Well, this is Miss Harding, and she is right handed."

The girl smiled at Hatch's astonishment.

"Then the other young woman merely impersonated Miss Harding?" he asked at last.

"That is all, and cleverly," replied The Thinking Machine. "She merely wanted me to read the cipher for her. I put her on the track of reading it herself purposely, and she and the persons associated with her are responsible for the excavation over there."

"But who is the other young woman?"

"She is the one who visited Miss Harding, wearing a mask."

"But what is her name?"

"I'm sure I haven't the faintest idea, Mr. Hatch," responded the little scientist shortly. "We have her to thank, however, for placing a solution of the affair into our hands. Who she is and in fact what she is, really is of no consequence, particularly as Miss Harding has this."

The scientist indicated the box with one small foot, then turned, and clambered into the waiting automobile.

4
THE PROBLEM OF THE STOLEN RUBENS

Matthew Kale made fifty million dollars out of axle grease, and afterward he began to patronize the high arts. It was simple enough: He had the money, and Europe had the old masters. His method of buying was simplicity itself. There were five thousand square yards of wall, more or less, in the huge gallery of his marble mansion which were to be covered, so he bought five thousand square yards, more or less, of art. Some of it was good, some of it fair, and much of it bad. The chief picture of the collection was a Rubens, which he had picked up for fifty thousand dollars in Rome.

Soon after acquiring his collection, Kale decided to make certain alterations in the vast room where the pictures hung. They were all taken down and stored in the ballroom, equally vast, with their faces toward the wall. Meanwhile Kale and his family took refuge in a nearby hotel.

It was at this hotel that Kale met Jules de Lesseps. De Lesseps was distinctly French, the sort of Frenchman whose conversation resembles calisthenics. He was nervous, quick, and agile, and he told Kale in confidence that he was not only a painter himself, but also a connoisseur of the high arts. Pompous in the pride of possession, Kale went to great lengths to exhibit his private collection for de Lesseps's enjoyment. It happened in the ballroom, and the true artist's delight shone in the Frenchman's eyes as he handled the pieces which were good. Some of the others made him smile, but it was an inoffensive sort of smile.

With his own hands Kale lifted the precious Rubens and held it before the Frenchman's eyes. It was a *Madonna and Child*, one of those wonderful creations which have endured through the years with all the sparkle and color beauty of their pristine days. Kale seemed disappointed because de Lesseps was not particularly enthusiastic about this picture.

"Why, it's a Rubens!" he exclaimed.

"Yes, I see," replied de Lesseps.

"It cost me fifty thousand dollars."

"It is perhaps worth more than that," and the Frenchman shrugged his shoulders as he turned away.

Kale looked at him in chagrin. Could it be that de Lesseps did not understand that it was a Rubens, or that Rubens was a painter? Or was it that he had failed to hear him say that it cost him fifty thousand dollars? Kale was accustomed to seeing people bob their heads and open their eyes when he said *fifty thousand dollars*; therefore, "Don't you like it?" he asked.

"Very much indeed," replied de Lesseps, "but I have seen it before. I saw it in Rome just a week or so before you purchased it."

They rummaged on through the pictures, and at last a Whistler was turned up for their inspection. It was one of the famous Thames series, a watercolor. De Lesseps's face radiated excitement, and several times he glanced from the watercolor to the Rubens as if mentally comparing the exquisitely penciled and colored modern work with the bold, masterly technique of the old.

Kale misunderstood the silence. "I don't think much of this one myself," he explained apologetically. "It's a Whistler, and all that. It cost me five thousand dollars, and I sort of had to have it, but still it isn't just the kind of thing that I like. What do you think of it?"

"I think it is perfectly wonderful!" replied the Frenchman enthusiastically. "It is the essence—the superlative—of modern work.

I wonder if it would be possible," and he turned to face Kale, "for me to make a copy of that? I have some slight skill in painting myself, and dare say I could make a fairly credible copy of it."

Kale was flattered. He was more and more impressed each moment with the picture. "Why, certainly," he replied. "I will have it sent up to the hotel, and you can—"

"No, no, no!" interrupted de Lesseps quickly. "I wouldn't care to accept the responsibility of having the picture in my charge. But if you would give me permission to come here—this room is large and airy and light, and besides it is quiet."

"Just as you like," said Kale magnanimously. "I merely thought the other way would be most convenient for you."

De Lesseps drew near and laid one hand on the millionaire's arm. "My dear friend," he said earnestly, "if these pictures were my pictures, I wouldn't try to accommodate anybody where they were concerned. I dare say the collection as it stands cost you—"

"Six hundred and eighty-seven thousand dollars," volunteered Kale proudly.

"And surely they must be well protected here in your house during your absence?"

"There are about twenty servants in the house while the workmen are making the alterations," said Kale, "and three of them don't do anything but watch this room. No one can go in or out except by the door we entered—the others are locked and barred—and then only with my permission or a written order from me. No, sir, nobody can get away with anything in this room."

"Excellent. Excellent!" said de Lesseps admiringly. He smiled a little bit. "I am afraid I did not give you credit for being the far-sighted businessman that you are." He turned and glanced over the collection of pictures abstractedly. "A clever thief, though," he ventured, "might cut a valuable painting, for instance the Rubens, out of the frame, roll it up, conceal it under his coat, and escape."

Kale laughed pleasantly and shook his head.

It was a couple of days later at the hotel that de Lesseps again brought up the subject of copying the Whistler. He was profuse in his thanks when Kale volunteered to accompany him to the mansion and witness the preliminary stages of the work. They paused at the ballroom door.

"Jennings," said Kale to the liveried servant there, "this is Mr. de Lesseps. He is to come and go as he likes. He is going to do some work in the ballroom here. See that he isn't disturbed."

De Lesseps noticed the Rubens leaning carelessly against some other pictures with the face of the Madonna toward them. "Really, Mr. Kale," he protested, "that picture is too valuable to be left about like that. If you will let your servants bring me some canvas, I shall wrap it and place it up on the table here off the floor. Suppose there were mice here!"

Kale thanked him. The necessary orders were given, and finally the picture was carefully wrapped and placed beyond harm's reach, whereupon de Lesseps adjusted himself, paper, easel, stool, and all, and began his work of copying. There Kale left him.

Three days later Kale just happened to drop in and found the artist still at his labor.

"I just dropped by," he explained, "to see how the work in the gallery was getting along. It will be finished in another week. I hope I am not disturbing you?"

"Not at all," said de Lesseps. "I have nearly finished. See how I am getting along?" He turned the easel toward Kale.

The millionaire gazed from that toward the original which stood on a chair near by, and frank admiration for the artist's efforts was in his eyes. "Why, it's fine!" he exclaimed. "It's just as good as the other one, and I bet you don't want any five thousand dollars for it—eh?"

That was all that was said about it at the time. Kale wandered about the house for an hour or so, then dropped into the ballroom where the artist was just getting his paraphernalia together, and they walked back to the hotel. The artist carried under one arm his copy of the Whistler, loosely rolled up.

Another week passed, and the workmen who had been engaged in refinishing and decorating the gallery had gone. De Lesseps volunteered to assist in the work of rehanging the pictures, and Kale gladly turned the matter over to him. It was in the afternoon of the day this work began that de Lesseps, chatting pleasantly with Kale, ripped loose the canvas which enshrouded the precious Rubens. Then he paused with an exclamation of dismay. The picture was gone; the frame which had held it was empty. A thin strip of canvas around the inside edge showed that a sharp penknife had been used to cut out the painting.

All of these facts came to the attention of Professor Augustus S. F. X. Van Dusen—The Thinking Machine. This was a day or so after Kale had rushed into Detective Mallory's office at police headquarters with the statement that his Rubens had been stolen. He banged his fist down on the detective's desk and roared at him.

"It cost me fifty thousand dollars!" he declared violently. "Why don't you do something? What are you sitting there staring at me for?"

"Don't excite yourself, Mr. Kale," the detective advised. "I will put my men to work right now to recover the . . . the . . . What is a Rubens anyway?"

"It's a picture!" bellowed Mr. Kale. "A piece of canvas with some paint on it, and it cost me fifty thousand dollars! Don't you forget that!"

So the police machinery was set in motion to recover the painting. And in time the matter fell under the watchful eye of Hutchinson Hatch, reporter. He learned the facts preceding the disappearance of the picture and then called on de Lesseps. He found the artist in a state of excitement bordering on hysteria. An intimation from the reporter of the object of his visit caused de Lesseps to burst into words.

"It is outrageous!" he exclaimed. "What can I do? I was the only one in the room for several days. I was the one who took such pains to protect the picture. And now it is gone! The loss is irreparable. What can I do?"

Hatch didn't have any very definite idea as to just what he could do, so he let him go on. "As I understand it, Mr. de Lesseps," he interrupted at last, "no one else was in the room except you and Mr. Kale all the time you were there?"

"No one else."

"And I think Mr. Kale said that you were making a copy of some famous watercolor, weren't you?"

"Yes, a Thames scene, by Whistler," was the reply. "That is it hanging over the mantel."

Hatch glanced at the picture admiringly. It was an exquisite copy and showed the deft touch of a man who was himself an artist of great ability.

De Lesseps read the admiration in his face. "It is not bad," he said modestly. "I studied with Carolus Duran."

With all else that was known, and this little additional information, which seemed of no particular value to the reporter, the entire matter was laid before The Thinking Machine. That distinguished man listened from beginning to end without comment.

"Who had access to the room?" he asked finally.

"That is what the police are working on now," was the reply. "There are a couple of dozen servants in the house, and I suppose, in spite of Kale's rigid orders, there was a certain laxity in their enforcement."

"Of course, that makes it more difficult," said The Thinking Machine in the perpetually irritated voice which was so distinctly a part of himself. "Perhaps it would be best for us to go to Mr. Kale's home and personally investigate."

Kale received them with the reserve which all rich men show in the presence of representatives of the press. He stared frankly and somewhat curiously at the diminutive figure of the scientist, who explained the object of their visit.

"I guess you fellows can't do anything with this," the millionaire assured them. "I've got some regular detectives on it."

"Is Mr. Mallory here now?" asked The Thinking Machine curtly.

"Yes, he is upstairs in the servants' quarters."

"May we see the room from which the picture was taken?" inquired the scientist with a suave intonation which Hatch knew so well.

Kale granted the permission with a wave of the hand and ushered them into the ballroom, where the pictures had been stored. From the relative center of this room, The Thinking Machine surveyed it all. The windows were high. Half a dozen doors leading out into the hallways, to the conservatory, and to quiet nooks of the mansion offered innumerable possibilities of access. After this one long comprehensive squint, The Thinking Machine went over and picked up the frame from which the Rubens had been cut. For a long time he examined it. Kale's impatience was painfully evident. Finally, the scientist turned to him.

"How well do you know Mr. de Lesseps?" he asked.

"I've known him for only a month or so. Why?"

"Did he bring you letters of introduction, or did you meet him merely casually?"

Kale regarded him with evident displeasure. "My own personal affairs have nothing whatever to do with this matter," he said pointedly. "Mr. de Lesseps is a gentleman of integrity, and certainly he is the last whom I would suspect of any connection with the disappearance of the picture."

"That is usually the case," remarked The Thinking Machine tartly. He turned to Hatch. "Just how good a copy was that he made of the Whistler picture?" he asked.

"I have never seen the original," Hatch replied, "but the workmanship was superb. Perhaps Mr. Kale wouldn't object to us seeing it."

"Oh, of course not," said Kale resignedly. "Come in. It's in the gallery."

Hatch submitted the picture to a careful scrutiny. "I should say that the copy is well-nigh perfect," was his verdict. "Of course, in its absence, I couldn't say exactly, but it is certainly a superb work."

The curtains of a wide door almost in front of them were thrown aside suddenly, and Detective Mallory entered. He carried something in his hand, but at the sight of them concealed it behind him. Unrepressed triumph was in his face.

"Ah, professor, we meet often, don't we?" he said.

"This reporter here and his friend seem to be trying to drag de Lesseps into this affair somehow," Kale complained to the detective. "I don't want anything like that to happen. He is liable to go out and print anything. They always do."

The Thinking Machine glared at him unwaveringly, straight in the eye for an instant and then extended his hand toward Mallory. "Where did you find it?" he asked.

"Sorry to disappoint you, professor," said the detective sarcastically, "but this is the time when you were a little late," and he produced the object which he held behind him. "Here is your picture, Mr. Kale."

Kale gasped a little in relief and astonishment and held up the canvas with both hands to examine it. "Fine!" he told the detective. "I'll see that you don't lose anything by this. Why, that thing cost me fifty thousand dollars!" Kale didn't seem able to get over that.

The Thinking Machine leaned forward to squint at the upper right hand corner of the canvas. "Where did you find it?" he asked again.

"Rolled up tight and concealed in the bottom of a trunk in the room of one of the servants," explained Mallory. "The servant's name is Jennings. He is now under arrest."

"Jennings!" exclaimed Kale. "Why, he has been with me for years."

"Did he confess?" asked the scientist imperturbably.

"Of course not," said Mallory. "He says some of the other servants must have hidden it there."

The Thinking Machine nodded at Hatch. "I think perhaps that is all," he remarked. "I congratulate you, Mr. Mallory, upon bringing the matter to such a quick and satisfactory conclusion."

Ten minutes later they left the house and caught a car for the scientist's home. Hatch was a little chagrined at the unexpected termination of the affair and was thoughtfully silent for a time.

"Mallory does show an occasional gleam of human intelligence, doesn't he?" he said at last quizzically.

"Not that I ever noticed," remarked The Thinking Machine crustily.

"But he found the picture," Hatch insisted.

"Of course, he found it. It was put there for him to find."

"Put there for him to find!" repeated the reporter. "Didn't Jennings steal it?"

"If he did, he's a fool."

"Well, if he didn't steal it, who put it there?"

"De Lesseps."

"De Lesseps!" echoed Hatch. "Why on earth did he steal a fifty thousand-dollar picture and put it in a servant's trunk to be found?"

The Thinking Machine twisted around in his seat and squinted at him coldly for a moment. "At times, Mr. Hatch, I am absolutely amazed at your stupidity," he said frankly. "I can understand it in a man like Mallory, but I have always given you credit for being an astute, quick-witted man."

Hatch smiled at the reproach. It was not the first time he had heard it. But nothing bearing on the problem at hand was said until they reached The Thinking Machine's apartment.

"The only real question in my mind, Mr. Hatch," said the scientist then, "is whether or not I should take the trouble to restore Mr. Kale's picture at all. He is perfectly satisfied and will probably never know the difference. So . . ."

Suddenly Hatch understood. "Do you mean that the picture that Mallory found was—"

"A copy of the original," supplemented the scientist. "Personally I know nothing whatever about art; therefore, I could not say from

71

observation that it is a copy, but I know it from the logic of the thing. When the original was cut from the frame, the knife swerved a little at the upper right-hand corner. The canvas remaining in the frame told me that. The picture that Mr. Mallory found did not correspond in this detail with the canvas in the frame. The conclusion is obvious."

"And de Lesseps has the original?"

"De Lesseps has the original. How did he get it? In any one of a dozen ways. He might have rolled it up and stuck it under his coat. He might have had a confederate. But I don't think that any ordinary method of theft would have appealed to him. I am giving him credit for being clever, as I must when we review the whole case.

"For instance, he asked for permission to copy the Whistler, which you saw was the same size as the Rubens. It was granted. He copied it practically under guard, always with the chance that Mr. Kale himself would drop in. It took him three days to copy it, so he says. He was alone in the room all that time. He knew that Mr. Kale had not the faintest idea of art. Taking advantage of that, what would have been simpler than to have copied the Rubens in oil? He could have removed it from the frame immediately after he covered it over, and kept it in a position near him where it could be quickly concealed if he was interrupted. Remember, the picture is worth fifty thousand dollars, therefore it was worth the trouble.

"De Lesseps is an artist—we know that—and, dealing with a man who knew nothing whatever of art, he had no fears. We may suppose his idea all along was to use the copy of the Rubens as a sort of decoy after he got away with the original. You saw that Mallory didn't know the difference, and it was safe for him to suppose that Mr. Kale wouldn't. His only danger until he could get away gracefully was of some critic or connoisseur seeing the copy. His boldness we see readily in the fact that he permitted himself to discover the theft and that he discovered it after he had volunteered to assist Mr. Kale in the general work of rehanging the pictures in the gallery. Just how he put the picture in Jenning's trunk I don't happen to know. We can imagine many ways." He lay back in his chair for a minute without speaking, eyes steadily turned upward, fingers placed precisely tip to tip.

"The only thing remaining is to go get the picture. It is in de Lesseps's room now—you told me that—and so we know it is safe. I dare say he knows that if he tried to run away it would inevitably put him under suspicion."

"But how did he take the picture from the Kale home?" asked Hatch.

"He took it with him probably under his arm the day he left the house with Mr. Kale," was the astonishing reply.

Hatch was staring at him in amazement. After a moment the scientist arose and passed into the adjoining room, and the telephone rang. When he joined Hatch again, he picked up his hat, and they went out together.

De Lesseps was in when they arrived, and he received them immediately. They conversed about the case generally for ten minutes while the scientist's eyes were turned inquiringly here and there about the room. At last there came a knock on the door.

"It is Detective Mallory, Mr. Hatch," remarked The Thinking Machine. "Open the door for him."

De Lesseps seemed startled for just one instant and then quickly recovered. Mallory's eyes were full of questions when he entered.

"I should like, Mr. Mallory," began The Thinking Machine, "to call your attention to this copy of Mr. Kale's picture by Whistler—over the mantel here. Isn't it excellent? You have seen the original?"

Mallory grunted. De Lesseps's face, instead of expressing appreciation at the compliment, blanched suddenly, and his hands closed tightly. Again he recovered himself and smiled.

"The beauty of this picture lies not only in its faithfulness to the original," the scientist went on, "but also in the fact that it was painted under extraordinary circumstances. For instance, I don't know if you know, Mr. Mallory, that it is possible to so combine glue and putty and a few other commonplace things into a paste which would effectually blot out an oil painting and offer at the same time an excellent surface for watercolor work."

There was a moment's pause, during which the three men stared at him silently with singularly conflicting emotions depicted on their faces.

"This watercolor, this copy of Whistler," continued the scientist evenly, "is painted on such a paste as I have described. That paste in turn covers the original Rubens picture. It can be removed with water without damage to the picture, which is in oil, so that instead of a copy of the Whistler painting, we have an original by Rubens, worth fifty thousand dollars. That is true, isn't it, Mr. de Lesseps?"

There was no reply to the question. None was needed. It was an hour later, after de Lesseps was safely in his cell, that Hatch called up The Thinking Machine on the telephone and asked one question.

"How did you know that the watercolor was painted over the Rubens?"

"Because it was the only absolutely safe way in which the Rubens could be hopelessly lost to those who were looking for it, and at the same time perfectly preserved," was the answer. "I told you de Lesseps was a clever man, and a little logic did the rest. Two and two always make four, Mr. Hatch, not sometimes, but all the time."

5

THE TRAGEDY OF THE
LIFE RAFT

'Twas a shabby picture altogether—old Peter Ordway in his office: the man shriveled, bent, cadaverous, aquiline of feature, with skin like parchment, and cunning, avaricious eyes. The room was gaunt and curtainless, with smoke-grimed windows, dusty, cheerless walls, and threadbare carpet, worn through here and there to the rough flooring beneath. Peter Ordway sat in a swivel chair in front of an ancient roll-top desk. Opposite, at a typewriter upon a table of early vintage, was his secretary—one Walpole, almost a replica in middle age of his employer, seedy and servile, with lips curled sneeringly as a dog's.

Familiar to those in the financial district, Peter Ordway was "The Usurer," a title which was at once a compliment to his merciless business sagacity and an expression of contempt for his methods. He was the money lender of the Street, holding in cash millions which no one dared to estimate. In the last big panic the richest man in America, the great John Morton in person, had spent hours in the shabby office, begging for the loan of the few millions in currency necessary to check the market. Peter Ordway didn't fail to take full advantage of his pressing need. Mr. Morton got the millions on collateral worth five times the sum borrowed, but Peter Ordway fixed the rate of interest, a staggering load.

Now we have the old man at the beginning of a day's work. After glancing through two or three letters which lay open on his desk, he picked up at last a white card, across the face of which was scribbled in pencil three words only:

One million dollars!

Ordinarily it was a phrase to bring a smile to his withered lips, a morsel to roll under his wicked old tongue; but now he stared at it without comprehension. Finally he turned to his secretary, Walpole.

"What is this?" he demanded querulously, in his thin, rasping voice.

"I don't know, sir," was the reply. "I found it in the morning's mail, sir, addressed to you."

Peter Ordway tore the card across and dropped it into the battered wastebasket beside him, after which he settled down to the ever-congenial occupation of making money.

On the following morning the card appeared again, with only three words, as before:

One million dollars!

Abruptly the aged millionaire wheeled around to face Walpole, who sat regarding him oddly.

"It came the same way, sir," the seedy little secretary explained hastily, "in a blank envelope. I saved the envelope, sir, if you would like to see it."

"Tear it up!" Peter Ordway directed sharply.

Reduced to fragments, the envelope found its way into the wastebasket. For many minutes Peter Ordway sat with dull, lusterless eyes, gazing through the window into the void of a leaden sky. Slowly, as he looked, he remembered.

The sky became a lashing, mist-covered sea, a titanic chaos of water. Upon its troubled bosom rode a life raft to which three persons were clinging. Now the frail craft was lifted up, up to the dizzy height of a giant wave; now it shot down sickeningly into the hissing trough beyond; again, for minutes it seemed altogether lost in the far-plunging spume. Peter Ordway shuddered and closed his eyes.

On the third morning the card, grown suddenly ominous, appeared again:

One million dollars!

Peter Ordway came to his feet with an exclamation that was almost a snarl, turning, twisting the white slip nervously in his talonlike fingers. Astonished, Walpole half arose, his yellow teeth bared defensively, and his eyes fixed upon the millionaire.

"Telephone Blake's Agency," the old man commanded, "and tell them to send a detective here at once."

In answer to the summons came a suave, smooth-faced, indolent young man, Fragson by name, who sat down after having regarded with grave suspicion the rickety chair to which he was invited. He waited inquiringly.

"Find the person—man or woman—who sent me that!"

Peter Ordway flung the card and the envelope in which it had come upon a leaf of his desk. Fragson picked them up and scrutinized them leisurely. Obviously the handwriting was that of a man, an uneducated man, he would have said. The postmark on the face of the envelope was Back Bay; the time of mailing seven p.m. on the night before. Both envelope and card were of a texture which might be purchased in a thousand shops.

"One million dollars!" Fragson read. "What does it mean?"

"I don't know," the millionaire answered.

"What do you think it means?"

"Nor do I know that, unless . . . unless it's some crank, or . . . or blackmailer. I've received three of them—one each morning for three days."

Fragson placed the card inside the envelope with irritating deliberation and thrust it into his pocket, after which he lifted his eyes quite casually to those of the secretary, Walpole. Walpole, who had been staring at the two men tensely, averted his shifty gaze and busied himself at his desk.

"Any idea who sent them?" Fragson was addressing Peter Ordway, but his eyes lingered lazily upon Walpole.

"No!" The word came emphatically, after an almost imperceptible instant of hesitation.

"Why," and the detective turned to the millionaire curiously, "why do you think it might be blackmail? Does anyone have any knowledge of any act of yours that—"

Some swift change crossed the parchmentlike face of the old man. For an instant he was silent and then his avaricious eyes leaped into flame. His fingers closed convulsively on the arms of his chair.

"Blackmail may be attempted without reason," he stormed suddenly. "Those cards must have some meaning. Find the person who sent them."

Fragson arose thoughtfully and drew on his gloves.

"And then?" he queried.

"That's all!" he said curtly. "Find him, and let me know who he is."

"Do I understand then that you don't want me to go into his motives? You merely want to locate the man?"

"That understanding is correct—yes."

. . . *a lashing, mist-covered sea, a titanic chaos of water. Upon its troubled bosom rode a life raft to which three persons were clinging. . . .*

Walpole's crafty eyes followed his millionaire employer's every movement as he entered his office on the morning of the fourth day. There was nervous restlessness in Peter Ordway's manner; the parchment face seemed more withered; the pale lips were tightly shut. For an instant he hesitated, as if vaguely fearing to begin on the morning's mail. But no fourth card had come. Walpole heard and understood the long breath of relief which followed upon realization of this fact.

Just before ten o'clock a telegram was brought in. Peter Ordway opened it:

One million dollars!

Three hours later at his favorite table in the modest restaurant where he always went for luncheon, Peter Ordway picked up his napkin, and a white card fluttered to the floor:

One million dollars!

Shortly after two o'clock a messenger boy entered his office, whistling, and laid an envelope on the desk before him:

One million dollars!

Instinctively he had known what was within.

At eight o'clock that night, in the shabby apartments where he lived with his one servant, he answered an insistent ringing of the telephone.

"What do you want?" he demanded abruptly.

The words came slowly, distinctly. "One million dollars!"

"Who are you?"

"One million dollars!" faintly, as an echo.

Again Fragson was summoned and was ushered into the cheerless room where the old millionaire sat cringing with fear, his face reflecting some deadly terror which seemed to be consuming him. Incoherently he related the events of the day. Fragson listened without comment and went out.

On the following morning, he returned to report. He found his client propped upon a sofa, haggard and worn, with eyes feverishly aglitter.

"Nothing doing," the detective began crisply. "It looked as if we had a clue which would at least give us a description of the man, but . . ." He shook his head.

"But that telegram. Some one filed it?" Peter Ordway questioned huskily. "The message the boy brought?"

"The telegram was enclosed in an envelope with the money necessary to send it and shoved through the mail slot of a telegraph office in Cambridge," the detective informed him explicitly. "That was Friday night. It was telegraphed to you on Saturday morning.

The card brought by the boy was handed in at a messenger agency by some street urchin, paid for, and delivered to you. The telephone call was from a public station in Brookline. A thousand persons use it every day."

For the first time in many years, Peter Ordway failed to appear at his office Monday morning. Instead he sent a note to his secretary: "Bring all important mail to my apartment tonight at eight o'clock. On your way uptown buy a good revolver with cartridges to fit."

Twice that day a physician, Dr. Anderson, was hurriedly summoned to Peter Ordway's side. First, there had been merely a fainting spell; later in the afternoon came complete collapse. Dr. Anderson diagnosed the case tersely.

"Nerves," he said. "Overwork and no recreation."

"But, Doctor, I have no time for recreation!" the old millionaire whined. "My business—"

"Time!" Doctor Anderson growled indignantly. "Time? You're seventy years old, and you're worth fifty million dollars. The thing you must have if you want to spend any of that money is an ocean trip—a good, long ocean trip—around the world if you like."

"No, no, no!" It was almost a shriek. Peter Ordway's evil countenance, already pallid, became ashen; abject terror was upon him.

. . . a lashing, mist-covered sea, a titanic chaos of water. Upon its troubled bosom rode a life raft to which three persons were clinging. . . .

"No, no, no!" he mumbled, his talon fingers clutching the physician's hand convulsively. "I'm afraid, afraid!"

The slender thread which held sordid soul to withered body was severed that night by a well-aimed bullet. Promptly at eight o'clock Walpole had arrived and gone straight to the room where Peter Ordway sat propped up on a sofa. Nearly an hour later the old millionaire's one servant, Mrs. Robinson, answered the doorbell, admitting Mr. Franklin Pingree, a well-known financier. He had barely stepped into the hallway when there came a reverberating crash as of a revolver shot from the room where Peter Ordway and his secretary were.

Together Mr. Pingree and Mrs. Robinson ran to the door. Still propped upon the couch, Peter Ordway sat—dead. A bullet had penetrated his heart. His head was thrown back, his mouth was open, and his right hand dangled at his side. Leaning over the body was his secretary, Walpole. In one hand he held a revolver, still smoking. He didn't turn as they entered, but stood staring down upon the man blankly. Mr. Pingree disarmed him from behind.

Hereto I append a partial transcript of a statement made by Frederick Walpole immediately following his arrest on the charge of murdering his millionaire employer. This statement he repeated in substance at the trial:

> *I am forty-eight years old. I had been in Mr. Ordway's employ for twenty-two years. My salary was eight dollars a week. . . . I went to his apartments on the night of the murder in answer to a note. [Note produced.] I bought the revolver and gave it to him. He loaded it and thrust it under the covering beside him on the sofa. . . . He dictated four letters and was starting on another. I heard the door open behind me. I thought it was Mrs. Robinson, as I had not heard the front door bell ring.*
>
> *Mr. Ordway stopped dictating, and I looked at him. He was staring toward the door. He seemed to be frightened. I looked around. A man had come in. He seemed very old. He had a flowing white beard and long white hair. His face was ruddy, like a seaman's.*
>
> *"Who are you?" Mr. Ordway asked.*
>
> *"You know me all right," said the man. "We were together long enough on that craft." [Or "raft," prisoner was not positive.]*
>
> *"I never saw you before," said Mr. Ordway. "I don't know what you mean."*
>
> *"I have come for the reward," said the man.*
>
> *"What reward?" Mr. Ordway asked.*

"One million dollars!" said the man.
Nothing else was said. Mr. Ordway drew his revolver
and fired. The other man must have fired at the same instant,
for Mr. Ordway fell back dead. The man disappeared. I ran
to Mr. Ordway and picked up the revolver. He had dropped
it. Mr. Pingree and Mrs. Robinson came in . . .

The reading of Peter Ordway's will disclosed the fact that he had bequeathed unconditionally the sum of one million dollars to his secretary, Walpole, for "loyal services." Despite Walpole's denial of any knowledge of this bequest, he was immediately placed under arrest.

At the trial, the facts appeared as I have related them. The district attorney summed them up briefly. The motive was obvious: Walpole's desire to get possession of one million dollars in cash. Mr. Pingree and Mrs. Robinson, entering the room directly after the shot had been fired, had met no one coming out, as they would have had there been another man. There was no other egress. Also they had heard only one shot, and that shot had found Peter Ordway's heart. The bullet which killed Peter Ordway had been positively identified by experts as of the same make and same caliber as those others in the revolver Walpole had bought. The jury was out twenty minutes. The verdict was guilty. Walpole was sentenced to death.

It was not until then that The Thinking Machine—Professor Augustus S. F. X. Van Dusen, PhD, FRS, MD, LLD, et cetera, et cetera, logician, analyst, mastermind in the sciences—turned his sullen genius upon the problem.

Five days before the date set for Walpole's execution, Hutchinson Hatch, newspaper reporter, introduced himself into The Thinking Machine's laboratory, bringing with him a small roll of newspapers. These two were old friends—on one hand, the man of science, small, almost grotesque in appearance, and living the life of a recluse; on the other, a young man of the world, enthusiastic, capable, and indefatigable.

So it came about that The Thinking Machine curled himself in a great chair and sat for nearly two hours partially submerged in newspaper accounts of the murder and of the trial. When at last he finished, he dropped his enormous head back against his chair, turned his petulant, squinting eyes upward, and sat for minute after minute staring into nothingness.

"Why," he queried at last, "do you think he is innocent?"

"I don't know that I do think it," Hatch replied. "It is simply that attention has been attracted to Walpole's story again because of a letter the governor received. Here is a copy of it."

The Thinking Machine read it:

You are about to allow the execution of an innocent man. Walpole's story on the witness stand was true. He didn't kill Peter Ordway. I killed him for a good and sufficient reason.

"Of course," the reporter explained, "the letter wasn't signed. However, three handwriting experts say it was written by the same hand that wrote the 'One million dollar' slips. Incidentally the prosecution made no attempt to connect Walpole's handwriting with those slips. They couldn't have done it, and it would have weakened their case."

"And what," inquired the diminutive scientist, "does the governor propose doing?"

"Nothing," was the reply. "To him this is merely one of a thousand crank letters."

"He knows the opinions of the experts?"

"He does. I told him."

"The governor," remarked The Thinking Machine gratuitously, "is a fool." Then: "It is sometimes interesting to assume the truth of the improbable. Suppose we assume Walpole's story to be true, assuming at the same time that this letter is true. What have we?"

Tiny, cobwebby lines of thought furrowed the domelike brow as Hatch watched. The slender fingers were brought precisely tip to tip; the pale blue eyes narrowed still more.

"If," Hatch pointed out, "Walpole's attorney had been able to find a bullet mark anywhere in that room or a single isolated drop of blood, it would have proven that Peter Ordway did fire as Walpole says he did, and—"

"If Walpole's story is true," The Thinking Machine went on serenely, heedless of the interruption, "we must believe that a man— say, Mr. X—entered a private apartment without ringing. Very well. Either the door was unlocked, he entered by a window, or he had a false key. We must believe that two shots were fired simultaneously, sounding as one. We must believe that Mr. X was either wounded or the bullet mark has been overlooked. We must believe Mr. X went out by the one door at the same instant Mr. Pingree and Mrs. Robinson entered. We must believe they either did not see him, or they lied."

"That's what convicted Walpole," Hatch declared. "Of course, it's impossible."

"Nothing is impossible, Mr. Hatch," stormed The Thinking Machine suddenly. "Don't say that. It annoys me exceedingly."

Hatch shrugged his shoulders and was silent. Again minute after minute passed, and the scientist sat motionless, staring now at a plan of Peter Ordway's apartment he had found in a newspaper; all the while his keen brain dissected the known facts.

"After all," he announced, at last, "there's only one vital question: Why Peter Ordway's deadly fear of water?"

The reporter shook his head blankly. He was never surprised anymore at The Thinking Machine's manner of approaching a problem. Never by any chance did he take hold of it as anyone else would have.

"Some personal eccentricity, perhaps," Hatch suggested hopefully. "Some people are afraid of cats, others of—"

"Go to Peter Ordway's place," The Thinking Machine interrupted tartly, "and find if it has been necessary to replace a broken windowpane anywhere in the building since Mr. Ordway's death."

"You mean, perhaps, that Mr. X, as you call him, may have escaped," the newspaperman began.

"Also find out if there was a curtain hanging over or near the door where Mr. X must have gone out."

"Right!"

"We'll assume that the room where Ordway died has been gone over inch by inch in the search for a stray shot," the scientist continued. "Let's go farther. If Ordway fired, it was probably toward the door where Mr. X entered. If Mr. X left the door open behind him, the shot may have gone into the private hall beyond and may be buried in the door immediately opposite." He indicated on the plan as he talked. "This second door opens into a rear hall. If both doors chanced to be open . . ."

Hatch came to his feet with blazing eyes. He understood. It was a possibility no one had considered. Ordway's shot, if he had fired one, might have lodged a hundred feet away.

"Then if we find a bullet mark," he questioned tensely.

"Walpole will not go to the electric chair."

"And if we don't?"

"We will look farther," said The Thinking Machine. "We will look for a wounded man of perhaps sixty years, who is now, or has been, a sailor; who is either clean-shaven or else has a close-cropped beard, probably dyed. A man who may have a false key to the Ordway apartment. The man who wrote this note to the governor."

"You believe, then," Hatch demanded, "that Walpole is innocent?"

"I believe nothing of the sort," snapped the scientist. "He's probably guilty. If we find no bullet mark, I'm merely saying what sort of man we must look for."

"But . . . but how do you know so much about him? What he looks like?" asked the reporter, in bewilderment.

"How do I know?" repeated the crabbed little scientist. "How do I know that two and two make four, not sometimes, but all the time? By adding the units together. Logic, that's all. Logic. Logic!"

While Hatch was scrutinizing the shabby walls of the old building where Peter Ordway had lived his miserly life, The Thinking Machine called on Dr. Anderson, who had been Peter Ordway's physician for a score of years. Dr. Anderson couldn't explain the old millionaire's aversion to water, but perhaps the scientist should go farther back in his inquiries. There was an old man, John Page, still living who had been Ordway's classmate in school. Dr. Anderson knew of him because he had once treated him at Peter Ordway's request. So The Thinking Machine came to discuss this curious trait of character with John Page. What the scientist learned didn't appear, but whatever it was, it sent him to the public library, where he spent several hours poring over the files of old newspapers.

All his enthusiasm gone, Hatch returned to report.

"Nothing," he said. "No trace of a bullet."

"Any windowpanes changed or broken?"

"Not one."

"There were curtains, of course, over the door through which Mr. X entered Ordway's room." It was not a question.

"There were. They're there yet."

"In that case," and The Thinking Machine raised his squinting eyes to the ceiling, "our sailor man was wounded."

"There is a sailor man, then?" Hatch questioned eagerly.

"I'm sure I don't know," was the astonishing reply. "If there is, he answers generally the description I gave. His name is Ben Holderby. His age is not sixty; it's fifty-eight."

The newspaper man took a long breath of amazement. Surely here was the logical faculty lifted to the nth power! The Thinking Machine was describing, naming, and giving the age of a man whose existence he didn't even venture to assert—a man who never had been in existence so far as the reporter knew! Hatch fanned himself weakly with his hat.

"Odd situation, isn't it?" asked The Thinking Machine. "It only proves that logic is inexorable, that it can only fail when the units fail; and no unit has failed yet. Meantime, I shall leave you to find

Holderby. Begin with the sailors' lodging houses, and don't scare him off. I can add nothing to the description except that he is probably using another name."

There followed a feverish two days for Hatch—a hurried, nightmarish effort to find a man who might or might not exist, in order to prevent a legal murder. With half a dozen other clever men from his office, he finally achieved the impossible.

"I've found him!" he announced triumphantly over the telephone to The Thinking Machine. "He's stopping at Werner's in the North End under the name of Benjamin Goode. He is clean-shaven, his hair and brows are dyed black, and he is wounded in the left arm."

"Thanks," said The Thinking Machine simply. "Bring Detective Mallory, of the Bureau of Criminal Investigation, and come here tomorrow at noon prepared to spend the day. You might go by and inform the governor, if you like, that Walpole will not be electrocuted Friday."

Detective Mallory came at Hatch's request—came with a mouthful of questions into the laboratory where The Thinking Machine was at work.

"What's it all about?" he demanded.

"Precisely at five o'clock this afternoon a man will try to murder me," the scientist informed him placidly, without lifting his eyes. "I'd like to have you here to prevent it."

Mallory was much given to outbursts of amazement, and he humored himself now.

"Who is the man? What's he going to try to kill you for? Why not arrest him now?"

"His name is Benjamin Holderby," The Thinking Machine answered the questions in order. "He'll try to kill me because I shall accuse him of murder. If he should be arrested now, he wouldn't talk. If I told you whom he murdered, you wouldn't believe it."

Detective Mallory stared without comprehension.

"If he isn't to try to kill you until five o'clock," he asked, "why send for me at noon?"

"Because he may know you, and if he watched and saw you enter, he wouldn't come. At half past four you and Mr. Hatch will step into the adjoining room. When Holderby enters, he will face me. Come behind him, but don't lift a finger until he threatens me. If you have to shoot, kill! He'll be dangerous until he's dead."

It was just two minutes before five o'clock when the bell rang, and Martha ushered Benjamin Holderby into the laboratory. He was past middle age, powerful, with a deeply-bronzed face and the keen eyes of the sea. His hair and brows were dyed—badly dyed; his left arm hung limply. He found The Thinking Machine alone.

"I got your letter, sir," he said respectfully. "If it's a yacht, I'm willing to ship as master; but I'm too old to do much."

"Sit down, please," the little scientist invited courteously, dropping into a chair as he spoke. "There are one or two questions I should like to ask. First," the petulant blue eyes were raised toward the ceiling. The slender fingers came together precisely, tip to tip. "First, why did you kill Peter Ordway?"

There fell an instant's amazed silence. Benjamin Holderby's muscles flexed, the ruddy face was contorted suddenly with hideous anger, the sinewy right hand closed tightly until great knots appeared in the tendons. Possibly The Thinking Machine had never been nearer death than in that moment when the sailor man towered above him—'twas giant and weakling. The tiger was about to spring. Then, as suddenly as it had come, anger passed from Holderby's face and became instead curiosity, bewilderment, perplexity.

The silence was broken by the sinister click of a revolver. Holderby turned his head slowly, to face Detective Mallory, stared at him oddly, then drew his own revolver, and passed it over, butt foremost.

No word had been spoken. Not once had The Thinking Machine lowered his eyes.

"I killed Peter Ordway," Holderby explained distinctly, "for good and sufficient reasons."

"So you wrote the governor," the scientist observed. "And your motive was born thirty-two years ago?"

"Yes." The sailor seemed merely astonished.

"On a raft at sea?"

"Yes."

"There was murder done on that raft?"

"Yes."

"Instigated by Peter Ordway, who offered you . . . ?"

"One million dollars. Yes."

"So Peter Ordway is the second man you have killed?"

"Yes."

With mouth agape, Hutchinson Hatch listened greedily; he had—they had—saved Walpole! Mallory's mind was a chaos. What sort of foolishness was this? This man was confessing to a murder for which Walpole was to be electrocuted! His line of thought was broken by the petulant voice of The Thinking Machine.

"Sit down, Mr. Holderby," he was saying, "and tell us precisely what happened on that raft."

'Twas a dramatic story Benjamin Holderby told, a tragic tale of the sea, a tale of starvation and thirst, torture and madness, and ceaseless battling for life, of crime and greed and the power of money even in that awful moment when death seemed the portion of all. The tale began with the foundering of the steamship *Neptune*, Liverpool to Boston, ninety-one passengers and crew, some thirty-two years ago. In mid-ocean she was smashed to bits by a gale and went down. Of those aboard, only nine persons reached shore alive.

Holderby told the story simply.

"No one knows how many of us went through that storm; it raged for days. There were ten of us on our raft when the ship settled, and by dusk of the second day there were only six—one woman, and a child, and four men. The waves would simply smash over us, and when we came to daylight again, there was someone missing. There was little enough food and water aboard anyway, so the people dropping off that way was really what saved . . . what saved two of us at the end. Peter Ordway was one, and I was the other.

"The first five days were bad enough—short rations, little or no water, no sleep, and all that—but what came after was horrendous! At the end of that fifth day there were only five of us: Ordway and me, the woman and child, and another man. I don't know if I went to sleep or was just unconscious; anyway, when I came to, there were only the three of us left. I asked Ordway where the woman and child was. He said they were washed off while I was asleep.

" 'And a good thing,' he says.

" 'Why?' I says.

" 'Too many mouths to feed,' he says. 'And still too many.' He meant the other man. 'I've been looking at the rations and water,' he says. 'There's enough to keep three people alive three days, but if there were only two people . . . me and you, for instance?' he says.

" 'You mean throw him off?' I says.

" 'You're a sailor,' says he. 'If you go, we all go. But we may not be picked up for days. We may starve or die of thirst first. If there were only two of us, we'd have a better chance. I'm worth millions of dollars,' he says. 'If you'll get rid of this other fellow, and we ever come out alive, I'll give you one million dollars!' I didn't say anything. 'If there were only two of us,' says he, 'we would increase our chances of being saved by one-third. One million dollars!' says he. 'One million dollars!'

"I expect I was mad with hunger and thirst and sleeplessness and exhaustion. Perhaps he was too. I know that, regardless of the money he offered, his argument appealed to me. Peter Ordway was a coward; he didn't have the nerve; so an hour later I threw the man overboard, with Peter Ordway looking on.

"Days passed somehow, and when I came to, I had been picked up by a sailing vessel. I was in an asylum for months. When I came out, I asked Ordway for money. He threatened to have me arrested for murder. I pestered him a lot, I guess, for a little later I found myself shanghaied on the high seas. I didn't come back for thirty years or so. I had almost forgotten the thing until I happened to see Peter Ordway's name in a paper. Then I wrote the slips and mailed them to him. He knew what they meant and set a detective after me. Then I began hating him all over again, worse than ever. Finally I thought I'd go to his house and make a holdup of it—one million dollars! I don't think I intended to kill him; I thought he'd give me money. I didn't know there was anyone with him. I talked to him, and he shot me. I killed him."

There fell a long silence. The Thinking Machine broke it, "You entered the apartment with a skeleton key?"

"Yes."

"And after the shot was fired, you started out but dodged behind the curtain at the door when you heard Mr. Pingree and Mrs. Robinson coming in?"

"Yes."

Suddenly Hatch understood why The Thinking Machine had asked him to ascertain if there were curtains at that door. It was quite possible that in the excitement Mr. Pingree and Mrs. Robinson would not have noticed that the man who killed Peter Ordway actually passed them in the doorway.

"I think," said The Thinking Machine, "that that is all. You understand, Mr. Mallory, that this confession is to be presented to the governor immediately, in order to save Walpole's life?" He turned to Holderby. "You don't want an innocent man to die for this crime?"

"Certainly not," was the reply. "That's why I wrote to the governor. Walpole's story was true. I was in court, and heard it." He glanced at Mallory curiously. "Now, if necessary, I'm willing to go to the chair."

"It won't be necessary," The Thinking Machine pointed out. "You didn't go to Peter Ordway's place to kill him. You went there for money you thought he owed you. He fired at you. You shot him. It's hardly self-defense, but it was not premeditated murder."

Detective Mallory whistled. It was the only satisfactory vent for the tangled mental condition which had befallen him. Shortly he went off with Holderby to the governor's office, and an hour later Walpole, deeply astonished, walked out of the death cell . . . a free man.

Meanwhile Hutchinson Hatch had some questions to ask of The Thinking Machine.

"Logic, logic, Mr. Hatch!" the scientist answered, in that perpetual tone of irritation. "As an experiment, we assumed the truth of Walpole's story. Very well. Peter Ordway was afraid of water. Connect that with the one word 'raft' or 'craft' in Walpole's statement of what the intruder had said. Then connect that with his description of that man—'ruddy, like a seaman.' Add them up, as you would a sum in arithmetic. You begin to get a glimmer of cause and effect, don't you? Peter Ordway was afraid of the water because of some tragedy there in which he had played a part. That was a tentative surmise. Walpole's description of the intruder said white hair and flowing white beard. It is a common failing of men who disguise themselves to go to the other extreme. I went to the other extreme in conjecturing Holderby's appearance—clean-shaven or else close-cropped beard and hair, dyed. Since no bullet mark was found in the building—remember, we are assuming Walpole's statement to be true—the man Ordway shot at carried the bullet away with him. Hence, a seaman with a pistol wound. Seamen, as a rule, stop at the sailors' lodging houses. That's all."

"But you knew Holderby's name—his age!" the reporter stammered.

"I learned them in my effort to account for Ordway's fear of water," was the reply. "An old friend, John Page, whom I found through Doctor Anderson, informed me that he had seen some account in a newspaper thirty-two years before, at the time of the wreck of the *Neptune*, of Peter Ordway's rescue from a raft at sea. He and one other man were picked up. The old newspaper files in the libraries gave me Holderby's name as the other survivor, together with his age. You found Holderby. I wrote to him that I was about to put a yacht in commission, and he had been recommended to me, that is, Benjamin *Goode* had been recommended. He came in answer to the advertisement. You saw everything else that happened."

"And the so-called 'one million dollar' slips?"

"Had no bearing on the case until Holderby wrote to the governor," said The Thinking Machine. "In that note he confessed the killing; I began to see that the 'one million dollar' slips probably indicated some enormous reward Ordway had offered Holderby. Walpole's statement, too, covers this point. What happened on the raft at sea? I didn't know. I followed an instinct and guessed." The distinguished scientist arose. "And now," he said, "be gone about your business. I must go to work."

Hatch started out but turned at the door. "Why," he asked, "were you so anxious to know if any windowpane in the Ordway house had been replaced or was broken?"

"Because," the scientist didn't lift his head, "because a bullet might have smashed one if it was not to be found in the woodwork. If it smashed one, our unknown Mr. X was not wounded."

Upon his own statement, Benjamin Holderby was sentenced to ten years in prison.

6
THE PHANTOM MOTOR

Two dazzling white lights bulged through the night as an automobile swept suddenly around a curve in the wide road and laid a smooth, glaring pathway ahead. Even at this distance the rhythmic *crackling-chug* informed Special Constable Baker that it was a gasoline car, and the headlong swoop of the unblinking lights toward him made him instantly aware of the fact that the speed ordinance of Yarborough County was being a little more than broken. It was being obliterated.

Now the County of Yarborough was a wide expanse of summer estates and superbly kept roads, level as a floor, which offered distracting temptations to the dangerous pastime of speeding. But against this was the fact that the county was particular about its speed laws—so particular in fact that it had stationed half a hundred men upon its highways to reduce the problem.

Incidentally, it had found that keeping record of the infractions of the law was an excellent source of income.

"Forty miles an hour if an inch," remarked Baker to himself. He arose from the stool where he sat watch from six o'clock until midnight, picked up his lantern, turned up the light, and stepped down to the edge of the road. He always remained on watch at the same place, at one end of a long stretch which drivers had dubbed "The Trap." The Trap was particularly tempting, a perfectly paved road lying between two tall stone walls, with only enough of a curving twist in it to make each end invisible from the other.

Another man, Special Constable Bowman, was stationed at the other end of The Trap, and there was telephone communication between the points, enabling the men to check each other. Incidentally, if one failed to stop a car or get its license number, the other would. That at least was the theory.

So now with the utmost confidence, Baker waited beside the road. The approaching lights were only a couple of hundred yards away. At the proper instant he would raise his lantern, the car would stop, its occupants would protest, and then the county would add a mite to its general fund for making the roads even better and tempting drivers still more. Sometimes the cars didn't stop. In that event it was part of the Special Constable's duties to get the number as it flew past. Referring to the automobile register would give the name of the owner. An extra fine was always imposed in such cases.

Without the slightest reduction of speed the car came hurtling toward him and swung wide so as to take the straightest path of The Trap at full speed.

At the desired instant Baker stepped out into the road and waved his lantern. "Stop!" he commanded. The *crackling-chug* came on, heedless of the cry. The auto was almost upon him before he leaped out of the road—a feat at which he was particularly expert—when it flashed by and plunged into The Trap. Baker was so busily engaged in getting out of the way that he didn't read the number, but he was not disconcerted because he knew there was no escape from The Trap.

On one side a solid stone wall eight feet high marked the eastern boundary of the John Phelps Stocker country estate, and on the other side a stone fence nine feet high marked the western boundary of the Thomas Q. Rogers country estate. There was no turnout, no place, no possible way for an auto to get out of The Trap except at one of the two ends guarded by the special constables.

So Baker, perfectly confident of results, seized the phone. "Car coming through at sixty miles an hour," he bawled. "It won't stop. I missed the number. Look out."

"All right," answered Special Constable Bowman.

For ten, fifteen, twenty minutes Baker waited expecting a call from Bowman at the other end. It didn't come, and finally he picked up the phone again. No answer. He rang several times, battered the box, and did some tricks with the receiver. Still no answer. Finally, he began to feel worried. He remembered that at that same post a Special Constable had been badly hurt by a reckless chauffeur who refused to stop or turn his car when the officer stepped out into the road. In his mind's eye he saw Bowman now lying helpless, perhaps badly injured. If the car held the pace at which it passed him, it would be certain death to whomever might be unlucky enough to get in its path.

With these thoughts running through his head and with genuine solicitude for Bowman, Baker walked along the road of The Trap toward the other end. The feeble rays of his lantern showed the un-broken line of cold, stone walls on each side. There was no shrub-bery of any sort, only a narrow strip of grass close to the wall. The more Baker considered the matter, the more anxious he became, and he increased his pace a little. As he turned a gentle curve, he saw a lantern in the distance coming slowly toward him. It was evi-dently being carried by someone who was looking carefully along each side of the road. "Hello!" called Baker when the lantern came within distance. "That you, Bowman?"

"Yes," came the hallooed response. The lanterns moved on and met.

Baker's solicitude for the other constable was quickly changed to curiosity. "What're you looking for?" he asked.

"That auto," replied Bowman. "It didn't come through my end, and I thought perhaps there had been an accident, so I walked along looking for it. Haven't seen anything."

"Didn't come through your end?" repeated Baker in amazement. "Why, it must have! It didn't come back my way, and I haven't passed it, so it must have gone through."

"Well, it didn't," declared Bowman conclusively. "I was on the lookout for it too. There hasn't been a car through my end in an hour."

Special Constable Baker raised his lantern until the rays fell full upon the face of Special Constable Bowman, and for an instant they stared at each other. Suspicion glowed from the keen, avaricious eyes of Baker. "How much did they pay you to let 'em by?" he asked.

"Pay me?" exclaimed Bowman, in righteous indignation. "Pay me nothing. I haven't seen a car."

A slight sneer curled the lips of Special Constable Baker. "Of course, but I happen to know that the auto came in here, that it didn't go back my way, that it couldn't get out except at the ends, therefore it went your way." He was silent for a moment. "And whatever extra money you got, Jim, seems to me I ought to get half."

Then the worm, Bowman, turned. A polite curl appeared about his lips and was permitted to show through the grizzled mustache. "I guess," he said deliberately, "you think that because you take bribes, everybody else does. I haven't seen any autos."

"Don't I always give you half, Jim?" Baker demanded, almost pleadingly.

"Well, I haven't seen any car, and that's all there is to it. If it didn't go back your way, there wasn't any car." There was a pause; Bowman was framing up something particularly unpleasant. "You're seeing things; that's what's the matter."

And so discord was sown between two officers of the County of Yarborough. After awhile they separated with mutual sneers and open derision and went back to their respective posts. Each was thoughtful in his own way.

At five minutes of midnight when they went off duty Baker called Bowman on the phone again. "I've been thinking this thing over, Jim, and I guess it would be just as well if we didn't report it or say anything about it when we go in," said Baker slowly. "It seems foolish, and if we did say anything it would give the boys a laugh on us."

"Just as you say," responded Bowman.

Relations between Special Constable Baker and Special Constable Bowman were strained on the morrow, but they walked along side by side to their respective posts. Baker stopped at his end of The Trap; Bowman didn't even look around.

"You'd better keep your eyes open tonight, Jim," Baker called as a last word.

"I had 'em open last night," was the disgusted retort.

Seven, eight, nine o'clock passed. Two or three cars had gone through The Trap at moderate speed, and one had been warned by Baker. At a few minutes past nine he was staring down the road which led into The Trap when he saw something that brought him quickly to his feet. It was a pair of dazzling lights, far away. He recognized them—the mysterious car of the night before. "I'll get it this time," he muttered grimly between closed teeth.

Then when the onrushing car was a full two hundred yards away, Baker planted himself in the middle of the road and began to swing the lantern. The auto seemed, if anything, to be traveling even faster than on the previous night. At a hundred yards Baker began to shout. Still the car didn't lessen speed but merely rushed on. Again at the desired instant Baker jumped. The auto whisked by as the chauffeur gave it a dextrous twist to prevent running down the Special Constable. Safely out of its way Baker, turned and stared after it, trying to read the number. He could see there was a number because a white board swung from the tail axle, but he could not make out the figures. Dust and a swaying car conspired to defeat him. But he did see that there were four persons in the car dimly silhouetted against the light reflected from the road. It was useless, of course, to conjecture more because even as he looked, the fast receding car swerved around the turn and was lost to sight.

Again he rushed to the telephone; Bowman responded promptly.

"That car's gone in again," Baker called. "Ninety miles an hour. Look out!"

"I'm looking," responded Bowman.

"Let me know what happens," Baker shouted.

With the receiver to his ear he stood for ten or fifteen minutes and then Bowman hallooed from the other end.

"Well?" Baker responded. "Get 'em?"

"No car passed through, and there's none in sight," said Bowman.

"But it went in," insisted Baker.

"Well, it didn't come out here," declared Bowman.

"Walk along the road till I meet you, and look out for it."

Then was repeated the search of the night before. When the two men met in the middle of The Trap, their faces were blank—blank as the high stone walls which stared at them from each side.

"Nothing!" said Bowman.

"Nothing!" echoed Baker.

Special Constable Bowman perched his head on one side and scratched his grizzly chin. "You're not trying to put up a job on me?" he inquired coldly. "You did see a car?"

"I certainly did," declared Baker, and a belligerent tone underlay his manner. "I certainly saw it, Jim, and if it didn't come out your end, why . . . why . . ." He paused and glanced quickly behind him. The action inspired a sudden similar caution on Bowman's part.

"Maybe . . . maybe . . ." said Bowman after a minute, "maybe it's a spook auto?"

"Well, it must be," mused Baker. "You know as well as I do that no car can get out of The Trap except at the ends. That car came in here; it isn't here now; it didn't go out your end. So where is it?"

Bowman stared at him a minute, picked up his lantern, shook his head solemnly, and wandered along the road back to his post.

On his way he glanced around quickly, apprehensively, three times. Baker did the same thing four times.

On the third night the phantom car appeared and disappeared precisely as it had done previously. Again Baker and Bowman met halfway between posts and talked it over.

"I'll tell you what, Baker," said Bowman in conclusion, "maybe you're just imagining that you see a car. Maybe if I was at your end, I wouldn't see it."

Special Constable Baker was distinctly hurt at the insinuation. "All right, Jim," he said at last, "if you think that way about it, we'll swap posts tomorrow night."

"Now that's the talk," exclaimed Bowman with an air approaching enthusiasm. "I'll bet I don't see it." On the following night Special Constable Bowman made himself comfortable on Special Constable Baker's stool, and he saw the phantom auto. It came upon him with a rush and a *crackling-chug* of engine and then sped on leaving him nerveless. He called Baker over the wire, and Baker watched half an hour for the phantom. It didn't appear.

Ultimately all things reach the newspapers, and so it was with the story of the phantom auto. Hutchinson Hatch, reporter, smiled incredulously when his city editor tersely stated the known facts. The known facts in this instance were meager almost to the disappearing point. They consisted of a corroborated statement that an automobile—solid and tangible enough to all appearances—rushed into The Trap each night and totally disappeared.

But there was enough of the bizarre about it to pique the curiosity and make one wonder, so Hatch journeyed down to Yarborough County, an hour's ride from the city, met and talked to Baker and Bowman, and then in broad daylight strolled along The Trap twice. It was a leisurely, thorough investigation with the end in view of finding out how an automobile once inside might get out again without going out either end.

On the first trip through Hatch paid particular attention to the Thomas Q. Rogers side of the road. The wall, nine feet high, was an unbroken line of stone with not the slightest indication of a secret driveway through it anywhere. Secret driveway! Hatch smiled at the phrase. But when he reached the other end, Bowman's end, of The Trap he was perfectly convinced of one thing—that no automobile had left the hard, paved road to go over, under, or through the Thomas Q. Rogers wall.

Returning, still leisurely, he paid strict attention to the John Phelps Stocker side, and when he reached the other end, Baker's end, he was convinced of another thing—that no automobile had left the road to go over, under, or through the John Phelps Stocker wall. The only opening of any sort was a narrow footpath, not more than sixteen inches wide. Hatch saw no shrubbery along the road, nothing but a strip of carefully tended grass, therefore the phantom auto could not be hidden any time, night or day. Hatch failed, too, to find any holes in the road, so the automobile didn't go down through the earth. At this point he involuntarily glanced up at the blue sky above. Perhaps, he thought whimsically, the automobile was a strange sort of bird, or . . . or . . . and he stopped suddenly. "I wonder if," he exclaimed. And the remainder of the afternoon he spent systematically making inquiries. He went from house to house, the Stocker house, the Rogers house, both of which were at the time unoccupied, then to cottage, cabin, and hut in turn. But he didn't seem overladen with information when he joined Special Constable Baker at his end of The Trap that evening about seven o'clock. Together they rehearsed the strange points of the mystery as the shadows grew about them until finally the darkness was so dense that Baker's lantern was the only bright spot in sight.

As the chill of the evening closed in, a certain awed tone crept into their voices. Occasionally an auto bowled along, and each time as it moved into sight Hatch glanced at Baker questioningly. And each time Baker shook his head. And each time, too, he called Bowman, in this manner accounting for every car that went into The Trap.

"It'll come all right," said Baker after a long silence, "and I'll know it the minute it rounds the curve coming toward us. I'd know its two lights in a thousand." They sat still and watched.

After a while two dazzling white lights burst into view far down the road and Baker, in excitement declared, "That's her. Look at her coming!"

And Hatch did look at her coming. The speed of the mysterious car was such as to make one look. Like the eyes of a giant the two lights came on toward them, and Baker perfunctorily went through the motions of attempting to stop it. The car fairly whizzed past them, and the rush of air which tugged at their coats was convincing enough proof of its solidity. Hatch strained his eyes to read the number as the auto flashed past. But it was hopeless. The tail of the car was lost in an eddying whirl of dust.

"She certainly does travel," commented Baker softly.

"She does," Hatch assented.

Then, for the benefit of the newspaper man, Baker called Bowman on the wire. "Car's coming again," he shouted. "Look out and let me know!"

Bowman, at his end, waited twenty minutes, then made the usual report. The car had not passed.

Hutchinson Hatch was a calm, cold, dispassionate young man, but now an odd, creepy sensation stole along his spinal column. He pulled himself together with a jerk. "There's one way to find out where it goes," he declared at last, emphatically, "and that's to place a man in the middle just beyond the bend of The Trap and let him wait and see. If the car goes up, down, or evaporates he'll see and can tell us."

Baker looked at him curiously. "I'd hate to be the man in the middle," he declared.

There was something of uneasiness in his manner.

"I rather think I would too," responded Hatch.

On the next evening, following the story of the phantom auto in Hatch's paper, there were twelve other reporters on hand. Most of them were openly, flagrantly skeptical; they even insinuated that no one had seen an auto.

Hatch smiled wisely. "Wait!" he advised with deep conviction.

So when the darkness fell that evening, the newspapermen of a great city had entered into a conspiracy to capture the phantom auto. Thirteen of them, making a total of fifteen men with Baker and Bowman, were on hand, and they agreed to a suggestion for all to take positions along the road of The Trap from Baker's post to Bowman's, watch for the auto, see what happened to it, and compare notes afterwards. So they scattered themselves along the road a few hundred feet apart and waited.

That night the phantom auto didn't appear at all, and twelve reporters jeered at Hutchinson Hatch.

The next night when Hatch and Baker and Bowman alone were watching the phantom auto reappeared.

Like a child with a troublesome problem, Hatch took the entire matter and laid it before Professor Augustus S. F. X. Van Dusen, the master brain. The Thinking Machine, with squinting eyes turned steadily upward and long, slender fingers pressed tip to tip, listened to the end.

"Now I know, of course, that automobiles don't fly," Hatch burst out savagely in conclusion, "and if this one doesn't fly, there is no earthly way for it to get out of The Trap, as they call it. I went over the thing carefully. I even went so far as to examine the ground and the tops of the walls to see if a runway had been let down for the auto to go over."

The Thinking Machine squinted at him inquiringly. "Are you sure you saw an automobile?" he demanded irritably.

"Certainly I saw it," blurted the reporter. "I not only saw it, I smelled it. Just to convince myself that it was real I tossed my cane in front of the thing, and it smashed it to toothpicks."

"Perhaps, then, if everything is as you say, the auto actually does fly," remarked the scientist.

The reporter stared into the calm, inscrutable face of The Thinking Machine, fearing first that he had not heard aright. Then he concluded that he had. "You mean," he inquired eagerly, "that the phantom may be an auto-airplane affair, and that it actually does fly?"

"It's not at all impossible," commented the scientist.

"I had an idea something like that myself," Hatch explained, "and questioned every soul within a mile or so, but I didn't get anything."

"The perfect stretch of road there might be the very place for some daring experimenter to get up sufficient speed to soar a short distance in a light machine," continued the scientist.

"Light machine?" Hatch repeated. "Did I tell you that this car had four people in it?"

"Four people!" exclaimed the scientist. "Dear me! Dear me! That makes it very different. Of course, four people would be too great a lift for an . . ."

For ten minutes he sat silent, and tiny cobwebby lines appeared in his dome-like brow. Then he arose and passed into the adjoining room. After a moment Hatch heard the telephone bell jingle. Five minutes later The Thinking Machine appeared and scowled at him unpleasantly. "I suppose what you really want to learn is if the car is a material one and to whom it belongs?" he queried.

"That's it," agreed the reporter, "and of course, why it does what it does, and how it gets out of The Trap."

"Do you happen to know a fast long-distance bicycle rider?" demanded the scientist abruptly.

"A dozen of them," replied the reporter promptly. "I think I see your idea, but . . ."

"You haven't the faintest inkling of my idea," declared The Thinking Machine positively. "If you can arrange with a fast rider who can go a distance—it might be thirty, forty, fifty miles—we may end this little affair without difficulty."

Under these circumstances Professor Augustus S. F. X. Van Dusen, PhD, LLD, FRS, MD, et cetera, et cetera, met the famous Jimmie Thalhauer, the world's champion long-distance bicyclist.

He held every record, had twice won the six-day race, and was altogether a master in his field. He came in chewing a toothpick. There were introductions.

"You ride the bicycle?" inquired the crusty little scientist.

"Well, some," confessed the champion modestly with a wink at Hatch.

"Can you keep up with an automobile for a distance of, say, thirty or forty miles?"

"I can keep up with anything that ain't got wings," was the response.

"Well, to tell you the truth," volunteered The Thinking Machine, "there is a growing belief that this particular automobile has wings. However, if you can keep up with it—"

"Ah, quit your kiddin'," said the champion, easily. "I can ride rings around anything on wheels. I'll start behind it and beat it where it's going."

The Thinking Machine examined the champion, Jimmie Thalhauer, as a curiosity. In the seclusion of his laboratory he had never had an opportunity of meeting just such another worldly young person. "How fast can you ride, Mr. Thalhauer?" he asked at last.

"I'm ashamed to tell you," confided the champion in a hushed voice. "I can ride so fast that I scare myself." He paused a moment. "But it seems to me," he said, "if there's thirty or forty miles to do I ought to do it on a motorcycle."

"Now that's just the point," explained The Thinking Machine. "A motorcycle makes noise and if it could have been used, we would have hired a fast automobile. This proposition briefly is: I want you to ride without lights behind an automobile which may also run without lights and find out where it goes. No occupant of the car must suspect that it is followed."

"Without lights?" repeated the champion.

"Yes, that's it," Hatch answered.

"I guess it's good for a four-column story? Huh?" inquired the champion. "Special pictures posed by the champion? Huh?"

"Yes," Hatch replied.

" 'Tracked on a Bicycle' sounds good to me. Huh?"

Hatch nodded.

So arrangements were concluded, and then and there The Thinking Machine gave definite and conclusive instructions to the champion. While these apparently bore on the problem in hand, they conveyed absolutely no inkling of his plan to the reporter. At the end the champion arose to go.

"You're a most extraordinary young man, Mr. Thalhauer," commented The Thinking Machine, admiring the sturdy, powerful figure.

And as Hatch accompanied the champion out the door and down the steps, Jimmie smiled with easy grace. "Nutty old guy, ain't he? Huh?"

Night! Utter blackness, relieved only by a white, ribbon-like road which winds away under a starless sky. Shadowy hedges line either side and occasionally a tree thrusts itself upward out of the somberness. The murmur of human voices in the shadows, then the *crackling-chug* of an engine, and an automobile moves slowly, without lights, into the road. There is the sudden clatter of an engine at high speed, and the car rushes away. From the hedge comes the faint rustle of leaves as of wind stirring. Then a figure moves impalpably. A moment and it becomes a separate entity—a quick movement and the creak of a leather bicycle saddle. Silently the single figure, bent low over the handlebars, moves after the car with ever-increasing momentum.

Then a long, desperate race. For mile after mile, mile after mile the auto goes on. The silent cyclist has crept up almost to the rear axle and hangs there doggedly as a racer to his pace. On and on they rush together through the darkness, the chauffeur moving with a perfect knowledge of his road, the single rider behind clinging on grimly with set teeth. The powerful, piston-like legs move up and down to the beat of the engine. At last, with dust-dry throat and stinging eyes the cyclist feels the pace slacken and instantly he drops back out of sight. It is only by sound that he follows now. The car stops; the cyclist is lost in the shadows. For two or three hours the auto stands deserted and silent. At last the voices are heard again, the car stirs, moves away and the cyclist drops in behind. Another race which leads off in another direction. Finally, from a knoll, the lights of a city are seen. Ten minutes elapse, the auto stops, the headlights flare up and more leisurely it proceeds on its way.

On the following evening The Thinking Machine and Hutchinson Hatch called upon Fielding Stanwood, President of the Fordyce National Bank. Mr. Stanwood looked at them with questioning eyes. "We called to inform you, Mr. Stanwood," explained The Thinking Machine, "that a box of securities, probably United States bonds, is missing from your bank."

"What?" exclaimed Mr. Stanwood, and his face paled. "Robbery?"

"I only know the bonds were taken out of the vault tonight by Joseph Marsh, your assistant cashier," said the scientist, "and that he, together with three other men, left the bank with the box and are now at a place I can name."

Mr. Stanwood was staring at him in amazement. "You know where they are?" he demanded.

"I said I did," replied the scientist shortly.

"Then we must inform the police at once, and . . ."

"I don't know that there has been an actual crime," interrupted the scientist. "I do know that every night for a week these bonds have been taken out through the connivance of your watchman and in each instance have been returned, intact, before morning. They will be returned tonight. Therefore I would advise, if you act, not to do so until the four men return with the bonds."

It was a singular party that met in the private office of President Stanwood at the bank just after midnight. Marsh and three companions, formally under arrest, were present as were President Stanwood, The Thinking Machine, and Hatch, besides detectives.

Marsh had the bonds under his arms when he was taken. He talked freely when questioned. "I will admit," he said without hesitating, "that I have acted beyond my rights in removing the bonds from the vault here, but there is no ground for prosecution. I am a responsible officer of this bank and have violated no trust. Nothing is missing; nothing is stolen. Every bond that went out of the bank is here."

"But why . . . why did you take the bonds?" demanded Mr. Stanwood.

Marsh shrugged his shoulders.

"It's what has been called a get-rich-quick scheme," said The Thinking Machine. "Mr. Hatch and I made some investigations today. Mr. Marsh and these other three are interested in a business venture which is ethically dishonest but which is within the law. They have sought backing for the scheme amounting to about a million dollars. Those four or five men of means with whom they have discussed the matter have called each night for a week at Marsh's country place. It was necessary to make them believe that there was already a million or so in the scheme, so these bonds were borrowed and represented to be owned by themselves. They were taken to and fro between the bank and his home in a kind of an automobile. This is really what happened, based on knowledge which Mr. Hatch has gathered and what I myself developed by the use of a little logic."

And his statement of the affair proved to be correct. Marsh and the others admitted the statement to be true.

It was while The Thinking Machine was homeward bound that he explained the phantom auto affair to Hatch. "The phantom auto, as you call it," he said, "is the vehicle in which the bonds were moved about. The phantom idea came merely by chance. On the night the vehicle was first noticed, it was rushing along to reach

Marsh's house in time for an appointment. A road map will show you that the most direct line from the bank to Marsh's was through The Trap. If an automobile should go half way through there, then out across the Stocker estate to the other road, distance would be lessened by a good five miles. This saving at first was, of course, valuable, so the car in which they rushed into The Trap was merely taken across the Stocker estate to the road in front."

"But how?" demanded Hatch. "There's no road there."

"I learned by phone from Mr. Stocker that there is a narrow walk from a very narrow foot gate in Stocker's wall on The Trap leading through the grounds to the other road. The phantom auto wasn't really an auto at all. It was merely two motorcycles arranged with seats and a steering apparatus. The French Army has been experimenting with them. The motorcycles are, of course, separate machines and as such it was easy to trundle them through a narrow gate and across to the other road. The seats are light; they can be carried under the arm."

"Oh!" exclaimed Hatch suddenly, then after a minute, "But what did Jimmie Thalhauer do for you?"

"He waited in the road at the other end of the footpath from The Trap," the scientist explained. "When the auto was brought through and put together, he followed it to Marsh's home and from there to the bank. The rest of it you and I worked out today. It's merely logic, Mr. Hatch, logic." There was a pause. "That Mr. Thalhauer is really a marvelous young man, Mr. Hatch, don't you think?"

7

THE PROBLEM OF THE STOLEN BANK NOTES

There was no mystery whatsoever about the identity of the man who, alone and unaided, robbed the Thirteenth National Bank of $109,437 in cash and $1.29 in postage stamps. It was Mort Dolan, an expert safecracker, albeit a young one, and he had made a clean sweep. Nor was there any mystery as to his whereabouts. He was safely in a cell at police headquarters, having been captured less than twelve hours after the robbery was discovered.

Dolan had offered no resistance to the officers when he was cornered, and he had attempted no denial when questioned by Detective Mallory. He knew he had been caught fair and squarely and no argument was possible, so he confessed, with a glow of pride at a job well done. It was four or five days after his arrest that the matter came to the attention of The Thinking Machine. Then the problem was . . .

But perhaps it is better to begin at the beginning.

Despite the fact that he was considerably less than thirty years old, Mort Dolan was a man for whom the police had a wholesome respect. He had a record, for he had started early. This robbery of the Thirteenth National Bank was his big job and was to have been his last. With the proceeds he had intended to take his wife and quietly disappear beneath a full beard and an alias to some place far removed from former haunts. But the mutability of human events is a matter of fact. While the robbery as a robbery was a thoroughly artistic piece of work and in full accordance with plans which had been worked out to the minutest details months before, Dolan had made one mistake. This was leaving behind him in the bank the can in which the nitroglycerin had been bought. Through this carelessness he had been traced.

Dolan and his wife occupied three small rooms in a poor tenement house. From the moment the police got a description of the person who bought the explosive, they were confident that they knew their man. Therefore, four clever men were on watch about the poor tenement. Neither Dolan nor his wife was there then, but from the condition of things in the rooms the police believed that they intended to return, so they took up positions to watch.

Unsuspecting enough, for his one mistake in the robbery had not occurred to him, Dolan came along just about dusk and started up the five steps to the front door of the tenement. It just happened that he glanced back and saw a head drawn suddenly behind a projecting stoop. But the electric light glared strongly there and Dolan recognized Detective Downey, one of many men who revolved around Detective Mallory within a limited orbit. Dolan paused on the stoop a moment while he thought it over. Perhaps instead of entering it would be best to stroll on down the street, turn a corner, and make a dash for it. But just at that moment he spied another head in the direction of contemplated flight. It was Detective Blanton.

Deeply thoughtful Dolan stared blankly in front of him. He knew of a back door opening onto the alley. Perhaps the detectives had not thought to guard that. He entered the house with affected unconcern and closed the door. Running lightly through the long, unclean hall which extended the full length of the building, he flung open the back door. He turned back instantly. Just outside he had seen and recognized Detective Cunningham.

Then he had an inspiration. The roof! The building was four stories. He ran up the four flights lightly but rapidly and was half way up the short flight which led to the opening in the roof when he stopped. From above he caught the whiff of a bad cigar, then the measured tread of heavy boots. Another detective! With a sickening depression at his heart Dolan came softly down the stairs again, opened the door of his flat with a key and entered.

Then and there he sat down to figure it all out. There seemed no escape for him. Every way out was blocked, and it was only a question of time before they would close in on him. He imagined now they were only waiting for his wife's return. He could fight for his freedom of course—even kill one, perhaps two, of the detectives who were waiting for him. But that would only mean his own death. If he tried to run for it past either of the detectives, he would get a shot in the back. But murder was repugnant to Dolan's artistic soul. It didn't do any good.

But could he warn Isabel, his wife? He feared she would walk into the trap as he had done, and she had had no connection of any sort with the affair. Then, from a fear that his wife would return, there swiftly came a fear that she would not. He suddenly remembered that it was necessary for him to see her. The police could not connect her with the robbery in any way; they could only hold her for a time and then would be compelled to free her, for her innocence of this particular crime was beyond question. And if he were taken before she returned, she would be left penniless. That was a thing which Dolan dreaded to contemplate. There was a spark of human tenderness in his heart and in prison it would be comforting to know that she was well cared for. If she would only come now, he would tell her where the money . . .

For ten minutes Dolan considered the question in all possible lights. A letter telling where the money was? No. It would inevitably fall into the hands of the police. A cipher? She would never get it. How? How? How? Every moment he expected a clamor at the door which would mean that the police had come for him. They knew he was cornered. Whatever he did must be done quickly. Dolan took a long breath and started to roll a cigarette. With the thin white paper held in his left hand and tobacco bag raised in the other he had an inspiration.

For a little more than an hour after that he was left alone. Finally his quick ear caught the shuffle of stealthy feet in the hall, then came an imperative rap on the door. The police had evidently feared to wait longer. Dolan was leaning over a sewing machine when the summons came. Instinctively his hand closed on his revolver, then he tossed it aside and walked to the door.

"Well?" he demanded.

"Let us in, Dolan," came the reply.

"That you, Downey?" Dolan inquired.

"Yes. Now don't make any mistakes, Mort. There are three of us here, and Cunningham is in the alley watching your windows. There's no way out."

For one instant—only an instant—Dolan hesitated. It was not that he was repentant; it was not that he feared prison; it was regret at being caught. He had planned it all so differently, and the little woman would be heartbroken. Finally, with a quick backward glance at the sewing machine, he opened the door. Three revolvers were thrust into his face with a unanimity that spoke well for the police opinion of the man. Dolan promptly raised his hands over his head.

"Oh, put down your guns," he expostulated. "I'm not crazy. My gun is over on the couch there."

Detective Downey, by a personal search, corroborated this statement. The revolvers were lowered.

"The chief wants you," he said. "It's about that Thirteenth National Bank robbery."

"All right," said Dolan calmly, and he held out his hands for the steel handcuffs.

"Now, Mort," said Downey ingratiatingly, "you can save us a lot of trouble by telling us where the money is."

"Doubtless I could," was the response.

Detective Downey looked at him and understood. Cunningham was called in from the alley. He and Downey remained in the apartment, and the other two men led Dolan away. In the natural course of events the prisoner appeared before Detective Mallory at police headquarters. They were well acquainted, professionally.

Dolan told everything frankly from the inception of the plan to the actual completion of the crime. The detective sat with his feet on his desk listening. At the end he leaned forward toward the prisoner.

"And where is the money?" he asked.

Dolan paused.

"That's my business," he responded, pleasantly.

"You might just as well tell us," insisted Detective Mallory. "We will find it, of course, and it will save us trouble."

"I'll just bet you don't find it," replied Dolan, and there was a glitter of triumph in his eyes. "On the level—between man and man now—I will bet you a hat that you never find that money."

"You're on," replied Detective Mallory. He looked keenly at his prisoner, and his prisoner stared back without a quiver. "Did your wife get away with it?"

From the question Dolan surmised that she had not been arrested.

"No," he answered.

"Is it in your flat?"

"Downey and Cunningham are searching now," was the rejoinder. "They will report what they find."

There was silence for several minutes as the two men—officer and prisoner—stared each at the other. When a thief refuses to answer questions, he becomes a difficult subject to handle. There was the third degree of course, but Dolan was the kind of man who would only laugh at that; the kind of man from whom anything less than physical torture could not bring a statement if he didn't choose to make it. Detective Mallory was perfectly aware of this dogged trait in his character.

"It's this way, chief," explained Dolan at last. "I robbed the bank, I got the money, and it's now where you will never find it.

I did it by myself, and I am willing to take my medicine. Nobody helped me. My wife—I know your men waited for her before they took me—my wife knows nothing on earth about it. She had no connection with the thing at all, and she can prove it. That's all I'm going to say. You might just as well make up your mind to it."

Detective Mallory's eyes snapped.

"You will tell where that money is," he blustered, "or . . . or I'll see that you get—"

"Twenty years is the absolute limit," interrupted Dolan quietly. "I expect to get twenty years. That's the worst you can do."

The detective stared at him hard.

"And besides," Dolan went on, "I won't be lonesome when I get where you're going to send me. I've got lots of friends there. Been there before. One of the jailers is the best pinochle player I ever met."

Like most men who find themselves thwarted at the outset, Detective Mallory sought to appease his indignation by heaping invective upon the prisoner, by threats, by promises, by wheedling, by bluster. It was all the same; Dolan remained silent. Finally he was led away and locked up.

A few minutes later Downey and Cunningham appeared. One glance told their chief that they could not enlighten him as to the whereabouts of the stolen money.

"Do you have any idea where it is?" he demanded.

"No, but I have a very definite idea where it isn't," replied Downey grimly. "It isn't in that flat. There's not one square inch of it that we didn't go over. Not one object there that we didn't tear to pieces looking. It simply isn't there. He hid it somewhere before we got him."

"Well, take all the men you want and keep at it," instructed Detective Mallory. "One of you, by the way, had better bring in Dolan's wife. I am fairly certain that she had nothing to do with it, but she might know something, and I can bluff a woman." Detective Mallory announced that accomplishment as if it were a thing to be proud of. "There's nothing to do now but get the money. Meanwhile I'll see that Dolan isn't permitted to communicate with anybody."

"There is always the chance," suggested Downey, "that a man as clever as Dolan could in a cipher letter, or by a chance remark, inform her where the money is if we assume she doesn't know. That should be guarded against."

"It will be guarded against," declared Detective Mallory emphatically. "Dolan will not be permitted to see or talk to anyone for the present. Not even an attorney. He may weaken later on."

But day followed day and Dolan showed no signs of weakening. His wife, meanwhile, had been apprehended and subjected to the third degree. When this ordeal was over, the net result was that Detective Mallory was convinced that she had had nothing whatever to do with the robbery, and had not the faintest idea where the money was. Half a dozen times Dolan asked permission to see her or to write to her. Each time the request was curtly refused.

Newspapermen, with and without inspiration, had sought the money vainly. The police were now seeking to trace the movements of Mort Dolan from the time of the robbery until the moment of his appearance on the steps of the house where he lived. In this way they hoped to get an inkling of where the money had been hidden, for the idea of the money being in the flat had been abandoned. Dolan simply wouldn't say anything.

Finally, Hutchinson Hatch, reporter, made an exhaustive search of Dolan's flat, for the fourth time, then went over to police headquarters to talk it over with Mallory. While there President Ashe and two directors of the victimized bank appeared. They were worried.

"Is there any trace of the money?" asked Mr. Ashe.

"Not yet," responded Detective Mallory.

"Well, could we talk to Dolan a few minutes?"

"If we didn't get anything out of him, you won't either," said the detective. "But it won't do any harm. Come along."

Dolan didn't seem particularly glad to see them. He came to the bars of his cell and peered through. It was only when Mr. Ashe was introduced to him as the president of the Thirteenth National that he seemed to take any interest in his visitors. This interest took the form of a grin. Mr. Ashe evidently had something of importance on his mind and was seeking the happiest method of expression. Once or twice he spoke aside to his companions, and Dolan watched them curiously. At last he turned to the prisoner.

"You admit that you robbed the bank?" he asked.

"There's no need of denying it," replied Dolan.

"Well," and Mr. Ashe hesitated a moment, "the board of directors held a meeting this morning, and speaking on their behalf I want to say something. If you will inform us of the whereabouts of the money, we will, upon its recovery, exert every effort within our power to have your sentence cut in half. In other words, as I understand it, you have given the police no trouble, you have confessed the crime. This, with the return of the money, would weigh for you when sentence is pronounced. Say the maximum is twenty years, we might be able to get you off with ten if we get the money."

Detective Mallory looked doubtful. He realized, perhaps, the futility of such a promise, yet he was silent. The proposition might draw out something on which to proceed.

"I can't see it," said Dolan at last. "It's this way. I'm twenty-seven years old. I'll get twenty years. About two of that'll come off for good behavior, so I'll really get eighteen years. At the end of that time I'll come out with one hundred and nine thousand dollars— rich for life and able to retire at forty-five years. In other words, while in prison I'll be working for a good, stiff salary—something really worth while. Very few men are able to retire at forty-five."

Mr. Ashe readily realized the truth of this statement. It was the point of view of a man to whom mere prison has few terrors—a man content to remain imprisoned for twenty years. He turned and spoke aside to the two directors again.

"But I'll tell you what I will do," said Dolan, after a pause. "If you'll fix it so I get only two years, I'll give you half the money."

There was silence. Detective Mallory strolled along the corridor beyond the view of the prisoner and summoned President Ashe to his side by a jerk of his head.

"Agree to that," he said. "Perhaps he'll really give up."

"But it wouldn't be possible to arrange it, would it?" asked Mr. Ashe.

"Certainly not," said the detective, "but agree to it. Get your money if you can, and then we'll nail him anyhow."

Mr. Ashe stared at him a moment vaguely indignant at the treachery of the thing, then greed triumphed. He walked back to the cell.

"We'll agree to that, Mr. Dolan," he said briskly. "Fix a two years' sentence for you in return for half the money."

Dolan smiled a little.

"All right, go ahead," he said. "When sentence of two years is pronounced and a first class lawyer arranges it for me so that the matter can never be reopened, I'll tell you where you can get your half."

"But you must tell us that now," said Mr. Ashe.

Dolan smiled cheerfully. It was a taunting, insinuating, accusing sort of smile, and it informed the bank president that the duplicity contemplated was discovered. Mr. Ashe was silent for a moment, then blushed.

"Nothing doing," said Dolan, and he retired into a recess of his cell as if his interest in the matter were at an end.

"But . . . but we need the money now," stammered Mr. Ashe. "It was a large sum, and the theft has crippled us considerably."

"All right," said Dolan carelessly. "The sooner I get two years, the sooner you get it."

"How could it be . . . be fixed?"

"I'll leave that to you."

That was all. The bank president and the two directors went out fuming impotently. Mr. Ashe paused in Detective Mallory's office long enough for a final word.

"Of course it was brilliant work on the part of the police to capture Dolan," he said caustically, "but it isn't doing us a particle of good. All I see now is that we lose a hundred and nine thousand dollars."

"It looks very much like it," assented the detective, "unless we find it."

"Well, why don't you find it?"

Detective Mallory had to give it up.

"What did Dolan do with the money?" Hutchinson Hatch was asking of Professor Augustus S. F. X. Van Dusen, The Thinking Machine. The distinguished scientist and logician was sitting with his head pillowed on a cushion and with squinting eyes turned upward. "It isn't in the flat. Everything indicates that it was hidden somewhere else."

"And Dolan's wife?" inquired The Thinking Machine in his perpetually irritated voice. "It seems conclusive that she had no idea where it is?"

"She has been put through the third degree," explained the reporter, "and if she had known, she would probably have told."

"Is she living in the flat now?"

"No. She is staying with her sister. The flat is under lock and key, and Mallory has the key. He has shown the utmost care in all he has done. Dolan has not been permitted to write to or see his wife for fear he would let her know in some way where the money is; he has not been permitted to communicate with anybody at all, not even a lawyer. He did see President Ashe and two directors of the bank, but naturally he wouldn't give them a message for his wife."

The Thinking Machine was silent. For five, ten, twenty minutes he sat with long, slender fingers pressed tip to tip, squinting unblinkingly at the ceiling. Hatch waited patiently.

"Of course," said the scientist at last, "one hundred and nine thousand dollars, even in large bills would make a considerable bundle and would be extremely difficult to hide in a place that has been gone over so often. We may suppose, therefore, that it isn't in the flat. What have the detectives learned as to Dolan's whereabouts after the robbery and before he was taken?"

"Nothing," replied Hatch, "absolutely nothing. He seemed to disappear off the earth for a time. That time, I suppose, was when he was disposing of the money. His plans were evidently well laid."

"It would be possible of course, by the simple rules of logic, to sit still here and ultimately locate the money," remarked The Thinking Machine musingly, "but it would take a long time. We might begin, for instance, with the idea that he contemplated flight? When? By rail or steamer? The answers to those questions would enlighten us as to the probable location of the money, because it would have to be placed where it was readily accessible in case of flight. But the process would be a long one. Perhaps it would be best to make Dolan tell us where he hid it."

"It would if he would tell," agreed the reporter, "but he is reticent to a degree that is maddening when the money is mentioned."

"Naturally," remarked the scientist. "But that really doesn't matter. I have no doubt he will inform me."

So Hatch and The Thinking Machine called upon Detective Mallory. They found him in deep abstraction. He glanced up at the intrusion with an appearance, almost, of relief. He knew intuitively what it was.

"If you can find out where that money is, Professor," he declared emphatically, "I'll . . . I'll . . . well, you can't."

The Thinking Machine squinted into the official eyes thoughtfully, and the corners of his straight mouth were drawn down disapprovingly.

"I think perhaps there has been a little too much caution here, Mr. Mallory," he said. "I have no doubt Dolan will inform me as to where the money is. As I understand it, his wife is practically without means?"

"Yes," was the reply. "She is living with her sister."

"And he has asked several times to be permitted to write to or see her?"

"Yes, dozens of times."

"Well, now suppose you do let him see her," suggested The Thinking Machine.

"That's just what he wants," blurted the detective. "If he ever sees her, I know he will, in some way, by something he says, by a gesture, or a look inform her where the money is. As it is now, I know she doesn't know where it is."

"Well, if he informs her, won't he also inform us?" demanded The Thinking Machine tartly. "If Dolan wants to convey knowledge of the whereabouts of the money to his wife, let him talk to her. Let him give her the information. I daresay, if she is clever enough to interpret a word as a clue to where the money is, I am too."

The detective thought that over. He knew this sullen little scientist with the enormous head of old, and he knew some of the amazing results he had achieved by methods wholly unlike those of the police. But in this case he was frankly in doubt.

"This way," The Thinking Machine continued. "Get the wife here, let her pass Dolan's cell and speak to him so that he will know that it is her, then let her carry on a conversation with him while she is beyond his sight. Have a stenographer, without the knowledge of either, take down just what is said, word for word. Give me a transcript of the conversation, and hold the wife on some pretext until I can study it a little. If he gives her a clue, I'll get the money."

There was not the slightest trace of egotism in the irritable tone. It seemed merely a statement of fact. Detective Mallory, looking at the wizened face of the logician, was doubtfully hopeful, and at last he consented to the experiment. The wife was sent for and came eagerly. A stenographer was placed in the cell adjoining Dolan, and the wife was led along the corridor. As she paused in front of Dolan's cell, he started toward her with an exclamation. Then she was led on a little way out of his sight.

With face pressed close against the bars Dolan glowered out upon Detective Mallory and Hatch. An expression of awful ferocity leapt into his eyes.

"What're you doing with her?" he demanded.

"Mort, Mort," she called.

"Belle, is it you?" he asked in turn.

"They told me you wanted to talk to me," explained the wife. She was panting fiercely as she struggled to shake off the hands which held her beyond his reach.

"What sort of a game is this, Mallory?" demanded Dolan.

"You've wanted to talk to her," Mallory replied, "now go ahead. You may talk, but you must not see her."

"Oh, that's it, eh?" snarled the prisoner. "What did you bring her here for then? Is she under arrest?"

"Mort, Mort," came his wife's voice again. "They won't let me come where I can see you."

There was utter silence for a moment. Hatch was overpowered by a feeling that he was intruding upon a family tragedy, and he tiptoed beyond reach of Dolan's roving eyes to where The Thinking Machine was sitting on a stool, twiddling his fingers. After a moment the detective joined them.

"Belle?" called Dolan again. It was almost a whisper.

"Don't say anything, Mort," she panted. "Cunningham and Blanton are holding me. The others are listening."

"I don't want to say anything," said Dolan easily. "I did want to see you. I wanted to know if you are getting along all right. Are you still at the flat?"

"No, at my sister's," was the reply. "I have no money. I can't stay at the flat."

"You know they're going to send me away?"

"Yes," and there was almost a sob in the voice. "I . . . I know."

"That I'll get the limit—twenty years?"

"Yes."

"Can you get along?" asked Dolan solicitously. "Is there any-thing you can do for yourself?"

"I will do something," was the reply. "Oh, Mort, Mort, why—"

"Oh never mind that," he interrupted impatiently. "It doesn't do any good to regret things. It isn't what I planned for, little girl, but it's here so I'll meet it. I'll get the good behavior allowance. That'll save two years. And then . . ."

There was a menace in the tone which was not lost upon the listeners.

"Eighteen years," he heard her moan.

For one instant Dolan's lips were pressed tightly together, and in that instant he had a regret—regret that he had not killed Blanton and Cunningham rather than submit to capture. He shook off his anger with an effort.

"I don't know if they'll permit me ever to see you," he said, desperately, "as long as I refuse to tell where the money is hidden, and I know they'll never permit me to write to you for fear I'll tell you where it is. So I suppose the goodbye'll be like this. I'm sorry, little girl."

He heard her weeping and hurled himself against the bars in a passion; it passed after a moment. He must not forget that she was penniless, and the money was a vast fortune!

"There's one thing you must do for me, Belle," he said after a moment, more calmly. "This sort of thing doesn't do any good. Brace up, little girl, and wait. Wait for me. Eighteen years is not forever, we're both young, and . . . but never mind that. I wish you would please go up to the flat and . . . do you remember my heavy, brown coat?"

"Yes, the old one?" she asked.

"That's the one," he answered. "It's cold here in this cell. Will you please go up to the flat when they let you loose and sew up that tear under the right arm and send it to me here? It's probably the last favor I'll ask of you for a long time, so will you do it this afternoon?"

"Yes," she answered, tearfully.

"The rip is under the right arm, and be certain to sew it up," said Dolan again. "Perhaps, when I am tried, I shall have a chance to see you and—"

The Thinking Machine arose and stretched himself a little. "That's all that's necessary, Mr. Mallory," he said. "Have her held until I tell you to release her."

Mallory made a motion to Cunningham and Blanton, and the woman was led away, screaming. Hatch shuddered a little, and Dolan, not understanding, flung himself against the bars of his cell like a caged animal.

"Clever, aren't you?" he snarled as he caught sight of Detective Mallory. "Thought I'd try to tell her where it was, but I didn't. You never will know where it is. Not in a thousand years."

Accompanied by The Thinking Machine and Hatch, the detective went back to his own office. All were silent, but the detective glanced from time to time into the eyes of the scientist.

"Now, Mr. Hatch, we have settled the whereabouts of the money," said Thinking Machine, quietly. "Please go at once to the flat and bring the brown coat Dolan mentioned. I daresay the secret of the hidden money is somewhere in that coat."

"But two of my men have already searched that coat," protested the detective.

"That doesn't make the least difference," snapped the scientist.

The reporter went out without a word. Half an hour later he returned with the brown coat. It was a common looking garment, badly worn and sadly in need of repair not only in the rip under the arm, but in other places. When he saw it, The Thinking Machine nodded his head abruptly as if it were just what he had expected.

"The money can't be in that," declared Detective Mallory, flatly. "There isn't room for it."

The Thinking Machine gave him a glance in which there was a touch of pity.

"We know," he said, "that the money isn't in this coat. But can't you see that it is perfectly possible that a slip of paper on which Dolan has written down the hiding place of the money can be hidden in it somewhere? Can't you see that he asked for this coat—which is not as good a one as the one he is wearing now—in order to attract his wife's attention to it? Can't you see it is the one definite thing that he mentioned when he knew that in all probability he would not be permitted to see his wife again, at least for a long time?"

Then, seam by seam, the brown coat was ripped to pieces. Each piece in turn was submitted to the sharpest scrutiny without result. Detective Mallory frankly regarded it all as wasted effort, and when there remained nothing of the coat save strips of cloth and lining, he was inclined to be triumphant. The Thinking Machine was merely thoughtful.

"It went further back than that," the scientist mused, and tiny wrinkles appeared in the domelike brow. "Ah! Mr. Hatch please go back to the flat, look in the sewing machine drawers, or work basket and you will find a spool of brown thread. Bring it to me."

"Spool of brown thread?" repeated the detective in amazement. "Have you been through the place?"

"No."

"How do you know there's a spool of brown thread there then?"

"I know it, because Mr. Hatch will bring it back to me," snapped The Thinking Machine. "I know it by the simplest, most rudimentary rules of logic."

Hatch went out again. In half an hour he returned with a spool of brown thread. The Thinking Machine's white fingers seized upon it eagerly, and his watery, squint eyes examined it. A portion of it had been used. The spool was only half gone. But he noted, and as he did his eyes reflected a glitter of triumph, that the paper cap on each end was still in place.

"Now, Mr. Mallory," he said, "I'll demonstrate to you that in Dolan the police are dealing with a man far beyond the ordinary bank thief. In his way he is a genius. Look here!"

With a penknife he ripped off the paper caps and looked through the hole of the spool. For an instant his face showed blank amazement. Then he put the spool down on the table and squinted at it for a moment in absolute silence.

"It must be here," he said at last. "It must be, else why did he—of course!"

With quick fingers he began to unwind the thread. Yard after yard it rolled off in his hand, and finally in the mass of brown on the spool appeared a white strip. In another instant The Thinking Machine held in his hand a tiny, thin sheet of paper—a cigarette paper. It had been wound around the spool and the thread wound over it so smoothly that it was impossible to see that it had ever been removed.

The detective and Hatch were leaning over his shoulder watching him curiously. The tiny paper unfolded. Something was written on it. Slowly The Thinking Machine deciphered it.

"47 Causeway Street, basement, tenth flagstone from northeast corner."

And there the money was found—one hundred and nine thousand dollars. The house was unoccupied and within easy reach of a wharf from which a European bound steamer sailed. Within half an hour of sailing time it would have been an easy matter for Dolan to have recovered it all, and that without in the least exciting the suspicion of those who might be watching him. A broken window in the basement gave quick access to the treasure.

"Dolan reasoned," The Thinking Machine explained, "that even if he was never permitted to see his wife, she would probably use that thread and in time find the directions for recovering the money. Further he argued that the police would never suspect that a spool contained the secret for which they sought so long. His conversation with his wife today was to draw her attention to something which would require her to use the spool of brown thread. The brown coat was all that he could think of. And that's all, I think."

Dolan was a sadly surprised man when news of the recovery of the money was broken to him. But a certain quaint philosophy didn't desert him. He gazed at Detective Mallory incredulously as the story was told and at the end went over and sat down on his cell cot.

"Well, chief," he said, "I didn't think it was in you. I owe you a hat."

8
THE PROBLEM OF THE CROSS MARK

It was an unsolved mystery, apparently a riddle without an answer, in which Watson Richards, the distinguished character actor, happened to play a principal part. The story was told at the Mummers Club one dull afternoon. Richards's listeners were three other actors, a celebrated poet, and a newspaper reporter named Hutchinson Hatch.

"You know there are very few men in the profession today who really amount to anything who haven't had their hard knocks. Well, my hard times came early and lasted a long time. So it was just about three years ago to a day that a real crisis came in my affairs. It seemed the end. I had gone one day without food, had bunked in the park that night, and here it was two o'clock in the afternoon of another day. It was dismal enough.

"I was standing on a corner, gazing moodily across the street at the display window of a restaurant, rapidly approaching the I-don't-care stage. Some one came up behind and touched me on the shoulder. I turned listlessly enough and found myself facing a stranger—a clean cut, well-groomed man of some forty years.

" 'Is this Mr. Watson Richards, the character actor?' he asked.

" 'Yes,' I replied.

" 'I have been looking for you everywhere,' he explained briefly. 'I want to engage you to do a part for one performance. Are you at liberty?'

"You chaps know what that meant to me just at that moment. Certainly the words dispelled some unpleasant possibilities I had been considering.

" 'I am at liberty. Yes,' I replied. 'Be glad to do it. What sort of part is it?'

" 'An old man,' he informed me. 'Just one performance, you know. Perhaps you'd better come uptown with me and see Mr. Hallman right now.'

"I agreed with a readiness which approached eagerness, and he called a passing cab. Hallman was perhaps the manager or stage manager, I thought. We had driven on for a block in the general direction of uptown, my companion chatting pleasantly. Finally, he offered me a cigar. I accepted it. I know now that cigar was drugged because I had hardly taken more than two or three puffs from it when I lost myself completely.

"The next thing I remember distinctly was stepping out of the cab—I think the stranger assisted me—and going into a house. I don't know where it was—I didn't know then—didn't know even the street. I was dizzy, giddy. And suddenly I stood before a tall, keen-faced, clean-shaven man. He was Hallman. The stranger introduced me and then left the room. Hallman regarded me keenly for several minutes, and somehow under that scrutiny my dormant faculties were aroused. I had thrown away the cigar at the door.

" 'You play character parts?' Hallman began.

" 'Yes, all the usual things,' I told him. 'I'm rather obscure, but—'

" 'I know,' he interrupted, 'but I have seen your work and like it. I have been told too that you are remarkably clever at makeup.'

"I think I blushed; I hope I did, anyway; I know I nodded. He paused to stare at me for a long time.

" 'For instance,' he went on finally, 'you would have no difficulty at all in making up as a man of seventy-five years?'

" 'Not the slightest,' I answered. 'I have played such parts.'

" 'Yes, yes, I know,' and he seemed a little impatient. 'Well, your makeup is the matter which is most important here. I want you for only one performance, but the makeup must be perfect, you understand.' Again he stopped and stared at me. 'The pay will be one hundred dollars for the one performance.'

"He drew out a drawer of a desk and produced a photograph. He looked at it, then at me, several times, and finally placed it in my hands.

" 'Can you make up to look precisely like that?' he asked.

"I studied the photograph closely. It was that of a man about seventy-five years old, of rather a long cast of features, not unlike the general shape of my own face. He had white hair and was clean-shaven. It was simple enough with the proper wig, a makeup box, and a mirror.

" 'I can,' I told Hallman.

" 'Would you mind putting on the makeup here now for my inspection?' he inquired.

" 'Certainly not,' I replied. It did not strike me at the moment as unusual. 'But I'll need the wig and paints.'

" 'Here they are,' said Hallman abruptly and produced them. 'There's a mirror in front of you. Go ahead.'

"I examined the wig and compared it with the photograph. It was as near perfect as I had ever seen. The makeup box was new and the most complete I ever saw. It didn't occur to me until a long time afterward that it had never been used before. So I went to work. Hallman paced up and down nervously behind me. At the end of twenty minutes I turned upon him a face which was so much like the photograph that I might have posed for it. He stared at me in amazement.

" 'By George!' he exclaimed. 'That's it! It's marvelous!' Then he turned and opened the door. 'Come in, Frank,' he called, and the man who had conducted me there entered. Hallman indicated me with a wave of his hand. 'How is it?' he asked.

"Frank, whoever he was, also seemed astonished. Then that passed, and a queer expression appeared on his face. You may imagine that I awaited their verdict anxiously.

" 'Perfect. Absolutely perfect,' said Frank at last.

" 'Perhaps the only thing,' Hallman mused critically, 'is that you aren't quite pale enough.'

" 'Easily remedied,' I replied, and turned again to the makeup box. A moment later I turned back to the two men. Simple enough, you know—it was one of those pallid, pasty-faced makeups like an old man on the verge of the grave—a good deal of pearl powder.

" 'That's it!' the two men exclaimed.

"The man Frank looked at Hallman inquiringly.

" 'Go ahead,' said Hallman, and Frank left the room.

"Hallman went over, closed and locked the door, after which he came back and sat down in front of me, staring at me for a long time in silence. At length he opened an upper drawer of the desk and glanced in. A revolver lay there, right under his hand. I know now he intended that I should see it.

" 'Now, Mr. Richards,' he said at last very slowly, 'what we want you to do is very simple, and as I said there's a hundred dollars in it. I know your circumstances perfectly. You need the hundred dollars.' He offered me a cigar, and foolishly enough I accepted it. 'The part you are to play is that of an old man, who is ill in bed, speechless, utterly helpless. You are dying, and you are to play the part. Use your eyes all you want, but don't speak.'

"Gradually the dizziness I had felt before was coming upon me again. As I said, I know now that it was the cigar, but I kept on smoking.

" 'There will be no rehearsal,' Hallman went on, and now I knew he was fingering the revolver I had seen in the desk, but it made no particular impression on me. 'If I ask you questions, you may nod an affirmative, but don't speak. Do only what I say, and nothing else.'

"Full realization was upon me now, but everything was growing hazy again. I remember I fought the feeling for a moment, then it seemed to overwhelm me, and I was utterly helpless under the dominating power of that man.

" 'When am I to play the part?' I remember asking.

" 'Now!' said Hallman suddenly, and he rose. 'I'm afraid you don't fully understand me yet, Mr. Richards. If you play the part properly, you get the hundred dollars; if you don't, this!'

"He meant the revolver. I stared at it dumbly, overcome by a helpless terror and tried to stand up. Then there came a blank, for how long I don't know. The next thing I remember I was lying in bed, propped up against several pillows. I opened my eyes feebly enough, and there wasn't any acting about it either because whoever drugged those cigars knew his business.

"There in front of me was Hallman. His grief stricken expression made all my art seem amateurish. There was another man there too, not Frank, and a woman who seemed to be about forty years old. I couldn't see their faces. I wouldn't even be able to suggest a description of them because the room was almost dark. Just the faintest flicker of light came through the drawn curtains. But I could see Hallman's devilish face all right. These three conversed together in low tones, sickroom voices, but I couldn't hear, and doubt if I could have followed their conversation if I had heard.

"Finally the door opened, and a girl entered. I have seen many women, but she was peculiarly fascinating. She gave one little cry, rushed toward the bed impulsively, dropped on her knees beside it, and buried her face in the sheets. She was shaking with sobs.

"Then I knew—intuitively, perhaps, but I knew—that in some way I was being used to injure that girl. A feeling of fearful anger seized upon me, but I couldn't move to save my soul. Hallman must have caught the blaze in my eyes, because he came forward on the other side of the bed and, under cover of a handkerchief which he had been using rather ostentatiously, pressed the revolver against my side.

"But I wouldn't be made a fool of. In my dazed condition I know I was seized with a desperate desire to fight it out—to make him kill me if he had to, but I would not deceive the girl. I knew if I could jerk my head down on the pillow it would disarrange the wig, and perhaps she would see. I couldn't. I might pass my hands across my makeup and smear it. But I couldn't lift my hands. I was struggling to speak and couldn't.

"Then somehow I lost myself again. Hazily I remember that somebody placed a paper in front of me on a book, a legal-looking document, and guided my hand across it, but that isn't clear. I was helpless, inert, so much clay in the hands of this man Hallman. Then everything faded . . . slowly, slowly. My impression was that I was actually dying; my eyelids closed of themselves; and the last thing I saw was the shining gold of that girl's hair as she sobbed there beside me.

"That's all of it. When I became fully conscious again, a policeman was shaking me. I was sitting on a bench in the park. He spoke to me loudly, and I got up and moved slowly along the path with my hands in my pockets. Something was clenched in one hand. I drew it out and looked at it. It was a hundred-dollar bill. I remember I got something to eat, and I woke up in a hospital.

"Well, that's the story. Make what you like of it. It can never be solved, of course. It was three years ago. You fellows know what I have done in that time. Well, I'd give it all, every bit of it, to meet that girl again. I would remember her, tell her what I know, and make her believe that it was no fault of mine."

Hutchinson Hatch related the circumstances casually a day or so later to Professor Augustus S. F. X. Van Dusen, The Thinking Machine.

That eminent man of science listened petulantly, as he listened to all things. "It happened in this city?" he inquired at the end.

"Yes."

"But Richards has no idea what part of the city?"

"Not the slightest. I imagine that the drugged cigar and a naturally weakened condition made him lose his bearings."

"I dare say," commented the scientist. "And, of course, he has never seen Hallman again?"

"No. He would have mentioned it if he had."

"Does Richards remember the exact date of the affair?"

"I dare say he does though he didn't mention it," replied the reporter.

"Suppose you see Richards and get the date—exactly, if possible," remarked The Thinking Machine. "You might telephone it to me. Perhaps . . ." and he shrugged his slender shoulders.

"You think there is a possibility of solving the riddle?" demanded the reporter eagerly.

"Certainly," snapped The Thinking Machine. "It requires no solution. It is ridiculously simple—obvious, I might say—and yet I dare say the girl Richards referred to has been the victim of some huge plot. It's worth looking into for her sake."

"Remember, it happened three years ago," Hatch suggested tentatively.

"It wouldn't matter particularly if it happened three hundred years ago," declared the scientist. "Logic, Mr. Hatch, remains the same through all the ages from Adam and Eve to us. Two and two made four in the Garden of Eden just as they do now in a counting house. Therefore, the solution, I say, is absurdly simple. The only problem is to discover the identity of the principals in the affair . . . and a child could do that."

Later that afternoon Hatch telephoned The Thinking Machine from the Mummers Club.

"That date you asked for was May 19, three years ago," said the reporter.

"Very well," commented The Thinking Machine. "Drop by tomorrow afternoon. Perhaps we can solve the riddle for Richards."

Hatch called late the following afternoon as directed, but The Thinking Machine was not in.

"He went out about nine o'clock and hasn't returned yet," the scientist's aged servant, Martha, informed him.

That night about ten o'clock Hatch used the telephone in a second attempt to reach The Thinking Machine.

"He hasn't come in yet," Martha told him over the wire. "He said he would be back for luncheon, but he isn't here yet."

Hatch replaced the receiver thoughtfully on the hook. Early the following morning he again used the telephone, and there was a note of anxiety in Martha's voice when she answered.

"He hasn't come yet, sir," she explained. "Please, what ought I to do? I'm afraid something has happened to him."

"Don't do anything yet," replied Hatch. "I dare say he'll return today."

Again at noon, at six o'clock, and at eleven that night Hatch called Martha on the telephone. Still the scientist had not appeared. Hatch too was worried now, yet how should he proceed? He didn't know, and he hesitated to think of the possibilities. On the morrow, however, something must be done. He would take the matter to Detective Mallory at police headquarters if necessary.

But this was unexpectedly made unnecessary by the arrival the next morning of a letter from The Thinking Machine. As Hatch read, an expression of utter bewilderment spread over his face. Tersely the letter was like this:

> *Employ an expert burglar, a careful, clever man. At two o'clock of the night following the receipt of this letter, go with him to the alley which runs behind Number 810 Blank Street. Enter this house with him from the rear, go up two flights of stairs, and let him pick the lock of the third door on the left from the head of the stairs. Silence above everything. Don't shoot if possible to avoid it.*
>
> *Van Dusen*
>
> *P.S. Put some ham sandwiches in your pocket.*

Hatch stared at the note in blank bewilderment for a long time, but he obeyed orders. Thus it came to pass that at ten minutes of two o'clock that night he boosted the notorious Blindy Bates—a man of rare accomplishments in his profession and at the moment happened to be out of prison—to the top of the rear fence of Number 810 Blank Street. Bates hauled up the reporter, and they leaped down lightly inside the yard.

The back door was simplicity itself to the gifted Bates and yielded in less than sixty seconds from the moment he laid his hand upon it. Then came a sneaking, noiseless advance along the hall to the accompaniment of innumerable thrills up and down Hatch's spinal column. Up the first flight safely with Blindy Bates leading the way, then along the hall and up the second flight. There was absolutely not a sound in the house. They moved like ghosts.

At the top of the second flight Bates shot a beam of light from his dark flashlight along the hall. The third door it was. And a moment later he was concentrating every faculty on the three locks of this door. Still there had been not the slightest sound. The one spot in the darkness was the bull's eye of the flashlight as it illuminated the lock. The first lock was unfastened, then the second, and finally the third. Bates didn't open the door. He merely stepped back, and the door opened as of its own volition. Involuntarily Hatch's hand closed fiercely on his revolver, and Bates's ready weapon glittered a little in the darkness.

"Thanks," came after a moment, in the quiet, querulous voice of The Thinking Machine. "Mr. Hatch, did you bring those sand-wiches?"

Half an hour later The Thinking Machine and Hatch appeared at police headquarters. Being naturally of a retiring, inconspicuous disposition, Bates did not accompany them; instead, he went his way fingering a bill of moderately large denomination.

Detective Mallory was at home in bed, but Detective Cunningham, another shining light, received his distinguished visitor and Hatch.

"There's a man named Howard Guerin now asleep in his state-room aboard the steamer *Austriana,* which sails at five o'clock this morning—just an hour and a half from now—for Hamburg," began The Thinking Machine without any preface. "Please have him arrested immediately."

"What charge?" asked the detective.

"Really, it's of no consequence," replied The Thinking Machine. "Attempted murder, conspiracy, embezzlement, fraud—whatever you like. I can prove any or all of them."

"I'll go after him myself," said the detective.

"There is also a young woman aboard," continued The Thinking Machine, "a Miss Hilda Fanshawe. Please have her detained, not arrested, and keep a close guard on her, not to prevent escape, but to protect her."

"Tell us some of the particulars of it," asked the detective.

"I haven't slept in more than forty-eight hours," replied The Thinking Machine. "I'll explain it all this afternoon after I've rested a while."

The Thinking Machine, for the benefit of Detective Mallory and his satellites, recited briefly the salient points of the story told by the actor, Watson Richards. His listeners were Howard Guerin, tall, keen-faced, and clean-shaven; Miss Hilda Fanshawe, whose pretty face reflected her every thought; Hutchinson Hatch; and three or four headquarters men. Every eye was upon the drawn face of the diminutive scientist, as he sat far back in his chair, with squinting eyes turned upward and fingertips pressed together.

"From the facts as he stated them, we know beyond all question that in the beginning Mr. Richards was used as a tool to further some conspiracy or fraud," explained The Thinking Machine. "That was obvious. So the first thing to do was to learn the identity of those persons who played the principal parts in it. From Mr. Richards's story we apparently had nothing, yet it gave us practically all of the names and addresses of the persons at the bottom of the thing.

"How? To find how, we'll have to consider the purpose of the conspiracy. An actor, an artist in facial impersonation, we might say, is picked up in the street and compelled to go through the pretense of a deathbed scene while stupefied with drugs. Obviously, this was arranged for the benefit of some person who must be convinced that he or she had witnessed a dissolution and the signature of a will, perhaps, a will signed under the eyes of that person for whose benefit the farce was acted.

"So we assume a will was signed. We know, within reason, that the scene was arranged for the benefit of a young woman, Miss Fanshawe here. From the intricacy and daring of the plot, it was pretty safe to assume that a large sum of money was involved. As a matter of fact, there was—more than a million dollars. Now, here is where we take an abstract problem and establish the identity of the actors in it. That will was signed by compulsory forgery, if I may use the phrase, by an utter stranger—a man who could not have known the handwriting of the man whose name he signed, and who was in a condition that makes it preposterous to imagine that he even attempted to sign that name. Yet the will was signed, and the conspirators had to have a signature that would bear inspection. Now, what have we left?

"When a person is incapable of signing his or her name, physically or by reason of no education, the law accepts a cross mark—an X—as a signature, when properly witnessed. We know Mr. Richards couldn't have known or imitated the signature of the old man he impersonated, but he did sign, therefore an X, which could have been established beyond question in a court of law. Now you see how I established the identity of the persons in this fraud. I got the date of the incident from Mr. Richards, then a trip to the surrogate's office told me all I wanted to know. What will had been filed for probate about that date that also bore the cross mark as a signature? The records answered the question instantly. John Wallace Lawrence.

"I glanced over the will. It specifically allowed Miss Hilda Fanshawe a trivial thousand dollars a year, and yet she was Lawrence's adopted daughter. See how the joints began to fit together? Further, the will left the bulk of the property to Howard Guerin, a

Mrs. Francis, since deceased by the way—and one Frank Hughes. The men were his nephews, the woman his niece. The joints continued to fit nicely. Therefore, the problem was solved. It was an easy matter to find these people, once I knew their names. I found Guerin, Mr. Richards knew him as Hallman, and asked him about the matter. From the fact that he locked me up in a room of his house and kept me prisoner for two days, I was convinced that he was the principal conspirator, and so it proves."

Again there was silence. Detective Mallory took three long breaths and asked a question. "But where was John Wallace Lawrence when this thing happened?"

"Miss Fanshawe had been in Europe and was rushing home, knowing that her adopted father was dying," The Thinking Machine explained. "As a matter of fact, when she returned, Mr. Lawrence was dead. He died the day before the farce which had been arranged for her benefit, and at that moment his body lay in an upstairs room. A day after the farce had been played, she attended his funeral. You see there was no reason why she should have suspected anything. I don't happen to know the provisions of Lawrence's real will, but I dare say it left practically everything to her. The thousand-dollar allowance by the conspirators was merely a sop to stop possible legal action."

The door of the room opened, and a uniformed man thrust his head in and announced "Mr. Richards wants to see Professor Van Dusen."

Immediately behind him came the actor. He stopped in the door and stared at Guerin for a moment.

"Why, hello, Hallman," he remarked pleasantly. Then his eyes fell upon the girl, and a flash of recognition lighted them.

"Miss Fanshawe, permit me. Mr. Richards," said The Thinking Machine. "You have met before. This is the gentleman you saw die."

"And where is Frank Hughes?" asked Detective Mallory.

"In South Africa," replied the scientist. "I learned a great deal while I was a prisoner."

A deeply troubled expression suddenly appeared on Hutchinson Hatch's face that night when he was writing the story for his newspaper, and he went to the telephone and called The Thinking Machine.

"If you were guarded so closely as a prisoner in that room, how on earth did you mail that letter to me?" he inquired.

"When Guerin came in to say some unpleasant things," came the reply, "he placed several letters he intended to post on the table for a moment. The letter for you was already written and stamped, and I was seeking a way to mail it, so I simply put it with his letters, and he mailed it for me."

Hatch burst out laughing.

9.
THE PROBLEM OF THE LOST RADIUM

One ounce of radium! Within his open palm Professor Dexter held practically the world's entire supply of that singular and seemingly inexhaustible force which was, and is, one of the greatest of all scientific riddles. So far as known there were only a few more grains in existence: four in the Curie laboratory in Paris, two in Berlin, two in St. Petersburg, one at Leland Stanford University, and one in London. All the remainder was here—here in the Yarvard laboratory, a tiny mass lumped on a small piece of steel.

Gazing at this vast concentrated power, Professor Dexter was a little awed and a little appalled at the responsibility which had suddenly fallen upon him, naturally enough with this culmination of a project which he had cherished for months. Briefly this had been to gather into one cohesive whole the many particles of the precious substance scattered over the world for the purpose of elaborate experiments as to its motive power practicability. Now here it was.

Its value, based on scarcity of supply, was incalculable. Millions of dollars would not replace it. Minute portions had come from the four quarters of the globe, in each case by special messenger, and each separate grain had been heavily insured by Lloyd's at a staggering premium. It was only after many months of labor, backed by the influence of the great University of Yarvard, in which he held the chair of physics, that Professor Dexter had been able to accomplish his purpose.

At least one famous name had been loaned to the proposed experiments, that of the distinguished scientist and logician, Professor Augustus S. F. X. Van Dusen, so called The Thinking Machine. The interest of this mastermind in the work was a triumph for Professor Dexter, who was young and comparatively unknown. The Thinking Machine, the elder scientist, was a court of last appeal in the sciences and from the moment his connection with Professor Dexter's plans was announced, his fellows all over the world had been anxiously awaiting a first word.

Naturally the task of gathering so great a quantity of radium had not been accomplished without extensive, and sometimes sensational, newspaper comment all over the United States and Europe. It was not astonishing, therefore, that news of the receipt of the final portion of the radium at Yarvard had been known in the daily press and with it a statement that Professors Van Dusen and Dexter would immediately begin their experiments.

The work was to be done in the immense laboratory at Yarvard, a high-ceilinged room with roof partially of glass and with windows set high in the walls far above the reach of curious eyes. Full preparations had been made; the two men were to work together, and a guard was to be stationed at the single door. This door led into a smaller room, a sort of reception hall, which in turn connected with the main hallway of the building.

Now Professor Dexter was alone in the laboratory, waiting impatiently for The Thinking Machine and turning over in his mind the preliminary steps in the labor he had undertaken. Every instrument was in place. All else was put aside for these experiments, which were either to revolutionize the motive power of the world or else demonstrate the utter uselessness of radium as a practical force.

Professor Dexter's line of thought was interrupted by the appearance of Mr. Bowen, one of the instructors of the university.

142

"A lady to see you, professor," he said as he handed him a card. "She said it was a matter of great importance to you."

Professor Dexter glanced at the card as Mr. Bowen turned and went out through the small room into the main hallway. The name, Madame Therese du Chastaigny, was wholly unfamiliar. Puzzled a little and perhaps impatient too, he carefully laid the steel with its burden of radium on the long table and started out into the reception room. Almost in the door he stumbled against something, recovered his equilibrium with an effort, and brought himself up with an undignified jerk.

The color mounted to his modest ears as he heard a woman laugh a pleasant, musical sort of ripple that under other circumstances would have been pleasant. Now being directed at his own discomfiture, it was irritating, and the Professor's face tingled a little as a tall woman arose and came towards him.

"Please pardon me," she said contritely, but there was still a flicker of a smile upon her red lips. "It was my carelessness. I should not have placed my suitcase in the door." She lifted it easily and replaced it in that identical position. "Or perhaps," she suggested inquiringly, "someone else coming out might stumble as you did?"

"No," replied the Professor, and he smiled a little through his blushes. "There is no one else in there."

As Madame du Chastaigny straightened up with a rustle of skirts to greet him, Professor Dexter was somewhat surprised at her height. She was apparently thirty years old and seemed from a casual glance, to be five feet nine or ten inches tall. In addition to a certain striking indefinable beauty, she was of remarkable physical power if one might judge from her poise and manner. Professor Dexter glanced at her and then at the card inquiringly.

"I have a letter of introduction to you from Madame Curie of France," she explained as she produced it from a tiny purse. "Shall we go over here where the light is better?"

She handed the letter to him, and together they seated themselves under one of the windows near the door to the outer hallway.

Professor Dexter pulled up a light chair facing her and opened the letter. He glanced through it and then looked up with a newly kindled interest in his eyes.

"I should not have disturbed you," Madame du Chastaigny explained pleasantly, "had I not known it was a matter of the greatest possible interest to you."

"Yes?" Professor Dexter nodded.

"It's radium," she continued. "It just happens that I have in my possession practically an ounce of radium of which the world of science has never heard."

"An ounce of radium!" repeated Professor Dexter incredulously. "Why, Madame, you astonish, amaze me. An ounce of radium?"

He leaned further forward in his chair and waited expectantly while the lady coughed violently. The paroxysm passed after a moment.

"That is my punishment for laughing," she explained smilingly. "I trust you will pardon me. I have a bad throat, and it was quick retribution."

"Yes, yes," said the other courteously, "but this other . . . it's most interesting. Please tell me about it."

Madame du Chastaigny made herself comfortable in the chair, cleared her throat, and began.

"It's rather an unusual story," she said apologetically, "but the radium came into my possession in quite a natural manner. I am English, so I speak the language, but my husband was French as my name indicates, and he, like you, was a scientist. He was little known to the world at large, however, as he was not connected with any institution. His experiments were undertaken for amusement, and they gradually led to a complete absorption of his interest. We were not wealthy as Americans count it, but we were comfortably well off.

"That much for my affairs. The letter I gave you from Madame Curie will tell you the rest as to who I am. Now when the discovery of this radium was made, my husband began some investigations along the same line, and they proved to be remarkably successful. His efforts were first directed towards producing radium, with what object, I was not aware at that time. Over the course of months he made grain after grain by some process unlike that of the Curies. Incidentally, he spent practically all our little fortune until he finally had nearly an ounce."

"Most interesting," commented Professor Dexter. "Please continue."

"It happened that during the production of the last quarter of an ounce, my husband contracted an illness which proved fatal." Madame du Chastaigny resumed after a slight pause, and her voice dropped. "I did not know the purpose of his experiments; I only knew what they had been and their comparative cost. On his deathbed he revealed this purpose to me. Strangely enough it was identical with yours as the newspapers have announced it, that is, the practicability of radium as a motive power. He was at work on plans looking to the utilization of its power when he died, but these plans were not perfected and unfortunately were in such shape as to be unintelligible to another."

She paused and sat silent for a moment. Professor Dexter watching her face, traced a shadow of grief and sorrow there, and his own big heart prompted a ready sympathy.

"And what," he asked, "was your purpose in coming to me now?"

"I know of the efforts you have made and the difficulties you have encountered in gathering enough radium for the experiments you have in mind," Madame du Chastaigny continued, "and it occurred to me that what I have, which is of no possible use to me, might be sold to you or to the university. As I said, there is nearly an ounce of it. It is where I can put my hands on it, and you, of course, are to make the tests to prove it is what it should be."

"Sell it?" gasped Professor Dexter. "Why, Madame, it's impossible. The funds of the college are not so plentiful that the vast fortune necessary to purchase such a quantity would be forthcoming."

A certain hopeful light in the face of the young woman passed, and there was a quick gesture of her hands which indicated disappointment.

"You speak of a vast fortune," she said at last. "I could not hope, of course, to realize anything like the actual value of the substance. A million perhaps? Only a few hundred thousands? Something to convert into available funds for me the fortune which has been sunk."

There was almost an appeal in her limpid voice, and Professor Dexter considered the matter deeply for several minutes as he stared out the window.

"Or perhaps," the woman hurried on after a moment, "it might be that you need more radium for the experiments you have in hand now, and there might be some sum paid me for the use of what I have? A sort of royalty? I am willing to do anything within reason."

Again there was a long pause. Ahead of him, with this hitherto unheard of quantity of radium available, Professor Dexter saw rosy possibilities in his chosen work. The thought gripped him more firmly as he considered it. He could see little chance of a purchase, but the use of the substance during his experiments! That might be arranged.

"Madame," he said at last, "I want to thank you deeply for coming to me. While I can promise nothing definite, I can promise that I will take up the matter with certain persons who may be able to do something for you. It's perfectly astounding. Yes, I may say that I will do something, but I shall perhaps, require several days to bring it about. Will you grant me that time?"

Madame du Chastaigny smiled.

"I must, of course," she said, and again she went off into a paroxysm of coughing, a distressing, hacking outburst which seemed to shake her whole body. "Of course," she added, when the spasm passed, "I can only hope that you can do something either in purchasing or using it."

"Could you fix a definite price for the quantity you have—that is a sale price—and another price merely for its use?" asked Professor Dexter.

"I can't do that offhand of course, but here is my address on this card. Hotel Teutonic. I expect to remain there for a few days, and you may reach me any time. Please, now please," and again there was a pleading note in her voice, and she laid one hand on his arm, "don't hesitate to make any offer to me. I shall be only too glad to accept it if I can."

She arose, and Professor Dexter stood beside her.

"For your information," she went on, "I will explain that I only arrived in this country yesterday by steamer from Liverpool, and my need is such that within another six months I shall be absolutely dependent upon what I may realize from the radium."

She crossed the room, picked up the suitcase and again she smiled, evidently at the recollection of Professor Dexter's awkward stumble. Then with her burden she turned to go.

"Permit me, Madame," suggested Professor Dexter, quickly, as he reached for the bag.

"Oh no, it is quite light," she responded easily.

There were a few commonplaces, and then she left. Gazing through the window after her, Professor Dexter stood deeply thoughtful for a minute considering the possibilities arising from her casual announcement of the existence of this unknown radium.

"If I only had that too," he muttered as he turned and reentered his work room.

An instant later, a cry—a wild amazed shriek—came from the laboratory, and Professor Dexter with pallid face rushed out through the reception room and flung open the door into the main hallway. Half a dozen students gathered about him and from across the hall Mr. Bowen, the instructor, appeared with startled eyes.

"The radium is gone—stolen!" gasped Professor Dexter.

The members of the little group stared at one another blankly while Professor Dexter raved impotently and ran his fingers through his hair. There were questions and conjectures; a babble was raging about him when a new figure loomed up in the picture. It was that of a small man with an enormous yellow head and an eternal petulant droop to the corners of his mouth. He had just turned a corner in the hall.

"Ah, Professor Van Dusen," exclaimed Professor Dexter, and he seized the long, slender hand of The Thinking Machine in a frenzied grip.

"Dear me! Dear me!" complained The Thinking Machine as he sought to extract his fingers from the vice. "Don't do that. What's the matter?"

"The radium is gone. Stolen!" Professor Dexter explained.

The Thinking Machine drew back a little and squinted aggressively into the distended eyes of his fellow scientist.

"Why that's perfectly silly," he said at last. "Come in, please, and tell me what happened."

With perspiration dripping from his brow and hands atremble, Professor Dexter followed him into the reception room, whereupon The Thinking Machine turned, closed the door into the hallway, and snapped the lock. Outside Mr. Bowen and the students heard the click and turned away to send the astonishing news hurtling through the great university. Inside Professor Dexter sank down on a chair with staring eyes and nervously twitching lips.

"Dear me, Dexter, are you crazy?" demanded The Thinking Machine irritably. "Compose yourself. What happened? What were the circumstances of the disappearance?"

"Come. Come in here to the laboratory and see," suggested Professor Dexter.

"Oh, never mind that now," said the other impatiently. "Tell me what happened."

Professor Dexter paced the length of the small room twice and then sat down again, controlling himself with a perceptible effort. Then, ramblingly but completely, he told the story of Madame du Chastaigny's call, covering every circumstance from the time he placed the radium on the table in the laboratory until he saw her drive away in the carriage. The Thinking Machine leaned back in his chair with squint eyes upturned and slender white fingers pressed tip to tip.

"How long was she here?" he asked at the end.

"Ten minutes, I should say," was the reply.

"Where did she sit?"

"Right where you are, facing the laboratory door."

The Thinking Machine glanced at the window behind him.

"And you?" he asked.

"I sat here facing her."

"You know that she did not enter the laboratory?"

"I know it, yes," replied Professor Dexter promptly. "No one save me has entered that laboratory today. I have taken particular pains to see that no one did. When Mr. Bowen spoke to me, I had the radium in my hand. He merely opened the door, handed me her card and went right out. Of course, it's impossible that—"

"Nothing is impossible, Mr. Dexter," blazed The Thinking Machine suddenly. "Did you at any time leave the lady in this room alone?"

"No, no," declared Dexter emphatically. "I was looking at her every moment she was here. I did not put the radium out of my hand until Mr. Bowen was out of this room and in the hallway there. I then came into this room and met her."

For several minutes The Thinking Machine sat perfectly silent, squinting upward while Professor Dexter gazed into the inscrutable face anxiously.

"I hope," ventured the Professor at last, "that you do not believe it was any fault of mine?"

The Thinking Machine did not say.

"What sort of a voice has Madame du Chastaigny?" he asked instead.

The Professor blinked a little in bewilderment.

"An ordinary voice. The low voice of a woman of education and refinement," he replied.

"Did she raise it at any time while talking?"

"No."

"Perhaps she sneezed or coughed while talking to you?"

Unadulterated astonishment was written on Professor Dexter's face.

"She coughed, yes, violently," he replied.

"Ah!" exclaimed The Thinking Machine and there was a flash of comprehension in the narrow blue eyes. "Twice, I suppose?"

Professor Dexter was staring at the scientist blankly.

"Yes, twice," he responded.

"Anything else?"

"Well, she laughed, I think."

"What was the occasion of her laughter?"

"I stumbled over a suitcase she had set down by the laboratory door there."

The Thinking Machine absorbed that without evidence of emotion and then reached for the letter of introduction which Madame du Chastaigny had given to Professor Dexter and which he still carried crumpled up in his hand. It was a short note, just a few lines in French, explaining that Madame du Chastaigny desired to see Professor Dexter on a matter of importance.

"Do you happen to know Madame Curie's handwriting?" asked The Thinking Machine after a cursory examination. "Of course, you had some correspondence with her about this work?"

"I know her writing, yes," was the reply. "I think that is genuine if that's what you mean."

"We'll see after a while," commented The Thinking Machine.

He arose and led the way into the laboratory. Professor Dexter indicated to him the exact spot on the worktable where the radium had been placed. Standing beside it, he made some mental calculation as he squinted about the room at the highly placed windows, the glass roof above, and the single door. Then wrinkles grew in his tall brow.

"I presume all the wall windows are kept fastened?"

"Yes, always."

"And those in the glass roof?"

"Yes."

"Then bring me a tall stepladder please."

It was produced after a few minutes. Professor Dexter looked on curiously and with a glimmer of understanding as The Thinking Machine examined each catch on every window and tapped the panes over with a penknife. When he had examined the last and found all locked, he came down the ladder.

"Dear me!" he exclaimed petulantly. "It's perfectly extraordinary. Most extraordinary. If the radium was not stolen through the reception room, then . . . then . . ." He glanced around the room again.

Professor Dexter shook his head. He had recovered his self-possession somewhat, but his bewilderment left him helpless.

"Are you sure, Professor Dexter," asked The Thinking Machine at last coldly, "are you sure you placed the radium where you have indicated?"

There was almost an accusation in the tone and Professor Dexter flushed hotly.

"I am positive, yes," he replied.

"And you are absolutely certain that neither Mr. Bowen nor Madame du Chastaigny entered this room?"

"I am absolutely positive."

The Thinking Machine wandered up and down the long table apparently without any interest, handling the familiar instruments and glittering appliances as a master.

151

"Did she happen to mention any children?" he at last asked, irrelevantly.

Professor Dexter blinked again.

"No," he replied.

"Adopted or otherwise?"

"No."

"Just what sort of a suitcase was it that she carried?"

"Oh, I don't know," replied Professor Dexter. "I didn't particularly notice. It seemed to be about the usual kind of a suitcase— leather, I imagine."

"She arrived in this country yesterday, you said?"

"Yes."

"It's perfectly extraordinary," The Thinking Machine grunted. Then he scribbled a line or two on a scrap of paper and handed it to Professor Dexter.

"Please have this sent by cable at once."

Professor Dexter glanced at it. It was:

Madame Curie, Paris:

Did you give Madame du Chastaigny letter of introduction for Professor Dexter? Answer quick.

Augustus S. F. X. Van Dusen

As Professor Dexter glanced at the dispatch his eyes opened a little.

"You don't believe that Madame du Chastaigny could have—" he began.

"I daresay I know what Madame Curie's answer will be," interrupted the other abruptly.

"What?"

"It will be no," was the positive reply. "And then . . ." He paused.

"Then . . . ?"

"Your veracity may be brought into question."

With flaming face and tightly clenched teeth but without a word, Professor Dexter saw The Thinking Machine unlock the door and leave. Then he dropped into a chair and buried his face in his hands. There Mr. Bowen found him a few minutes later.

"Ah, Mr. Bowen," he said, as he glanced up, "please have this cable sent immediately."

Once in his apartment, The Thinking Machine telephoned to Hutchinson Hatch, reporter, at the office of his newspaper. The young man was fairly bubbling with suppressed emotion when he rushed to answer the phone, and the exhilaration of pure enthusiasm made his voice vibrant when he spoke. The Thinking Machine readily understood.

"It's about the radium theft at Yarvard that I wanted to speak to you," he said.

"Yes," Hatch replied. "just heard of it this minute. A bulletin from police headquarters. I was about to go out on it."

"Please do something for me first," requested The Thinking Machine. "Go at once to the Hotel Teutonic and ascertain indisputably for me whether or not Madame du Chastaigny, who is staying there, is accompanied by a child."

"Certainly, of course," said Hatch, "but the story—"

"This is the story," interrupted The Thinking Machine tartly. "If you can learn nothing of any child at the hotel, go to the steamer on which she arrived yesterday from Liverpool and inquire there. I must have definite, absolute, indisputable evidence."

"I'm off," Hatch responded.

He hung up the receiver and rushed out. He happened to be professionally acquainted with the chief clerk of the Teutonic, a monosyllabic, rotund gentleman who was an occasional source of private information and who spent his life adding up a column of figures.

"Hello, Charlie," Hatch greeted him. "Madame du Chastaigny stopping here?"

"Yep," said Charlie.

"Husband with her?"

"Nope."

"By herself when she came?"

"Yep."

"Hasn't a child with her?"

"Nope."

"What does she look like?"

"Remarkable!" said Charlie.

This last loquacious outburst seemed to appease the reporter's burning thirst for information, and he rushed away to the dock where the steamship, *Granada* from Liverpool, still lay. Aboard he sought out the purser and questioned him along the same lines with the same result. There was no trace of a child. Then Hatch made his way to the home of The Thinking Machine.

"Well?" demanded the scientist.

The reporter shook his head.

"She hasn't seen or spoken to a child since she left Liverpool so far as I can ascertain," he declared.

It was not quite surprise; it was rather perturbation in the manner of The Thinking Machine now. It showed in a quick gesture of one hand, in the wrinkles on his brow, in the narrowing down of his eyes. He dropped back into a chair and remained there silent, thoughtful for a long time.

"It couldn't have been, it couldn't have been, it couldn't have been," the scientist broke out finally.

Having no personal knowledge on the subject, whatever it was, Hatch discreetly remained silent. After a while The Thinking Machine aroused himself with a jerk and related to the reporter the story of the lost radium so far as it was known.

"The letter of introduction from Madame Curie opened the way for Madame du Chastaigny," he explained. "Frankly, I believe that letter to be a forgery. I cabled asking Madame Curie. A 'no' from her will mean that my conjecture is correct; a 'yes' will mean . . . but that is hardly worth considering. The question now is: What method was employed to cause the disappearance of the radium from that room?"

The door opened, and Martha appeared. She handed a cablegram to The Thinking Machine, and he ripped it open with hurried fingers. He glanced at the sheet once, and then arose suddenly after which he sat down again, just as suddenly.

"What is it?" ventured Hatch.

"It's 'yes,' " was the reply.

In the seclusion of his own small laboratory The Thinking Machine was making some sort of chemical experiment about eight o'clock that night. He was just hoisting a graduated glass, containing a purplish, hazy fluid, to get the lamp light through it when an idea flashed into his mind. He permitted the glass to fall and smash on the floor.

"Perfectly stupid of me," he grumbled, and turning he walked into an adjoining room without so much as a glance at the wrecked glass. A minute later he had Hutchinson Hatch on the telephone.

"Come right up," he instructed.

There was something in his voice which caused Hatch to jump. He seized his hat and rushed out of his office. When he reached The Thinking Machine's apartment, that gentleman was just emerging from the room where the telephone was.

"I have it," the scientist told the reporter, forestalling a question. "It's ridiculously simple. I can't imagine how I missed it except through stupidity."

Hatch smiled behind his hand. Certainly stupidity was not to be charged against The Thinking Machine.

"Come in a cab?" asked the scientist.

"Yes, it's waiting."

"Come on then."

They went out together. The scientist gave some instruction to the cabby, and they clattered off.

"You're going to meet a very remarkable person," The Thinking Machine explained. "He may cause trouble, and he may not. Anyway, look out for him. He's tricky."

That was all. The cab drew up in front of a large building, evidently a boarding house of the middle class. The Thinking Machine jumped out, Hatch following, and together they ascended the steps. A maid answered the bell.

"Is Mr. . . . Mr. . . . oh, what's his name?" and The Thinking Machine snapped his fingers as if trying to remember. "Mr. . . . , the small gentleman who arrived from Liverpool yesterday . . ."

"Oh," the maid smiled broadly, "you mean Mr. Berkerstrom?"

"Yes, that's the name," exclaimed the scientist. "Is he in, please?"

"I think so, sir," said the maid, still smiling. "Shall I take your card?"

"No, it isn't necessary," replied The Thinking Machine.

"Second floor, rear," said the maid.

They ascended the stairs and paused in front of a door. The Thinking Machine tried it softly. It was unlocked, and he pushed it open. A bright light blazed from a gas jet, but no person was in sight. As they stood silent, they heard a newspaper rattle, and both looked in the direction whence came the sound.

Still no one appeared. The Thinking Machine raised a finger and tiptoed to a large upholstered chair which faced the other way. His slender hand disappeared around the side then lifted immediately, and wriggling in his grasp was a small man—a dwarf—a miniature man in a smoking jacket and slippers who protested fluently in German. Hatch burst out laughing, an uncontrollable fit which left him breathless.

"Mr. Berkerstrom, Mr. Hatch," said The Thinking Machine gravely. "This is the gentleman, Mr. Hatch, who stole the radium."

"Ach!" raged the little man. "Let me down, der chair in, ef you blease."

The Thinking Machine lowered the tiny wriggling figure back into the chair while Hatch closed and locked the door. When the reporter came back and looked, laughter was gone. The drawn wrinkled face of the man, the small body, the tiny clothing, added to the pitiful helplessness of the little figure. His age might have been fifteen or fifty, his weight was certainly not more than twenty-five pounds, his height barely thirty inches.

"It iss as we did him in der theatre, und . . ." Mr. Berkerstrom started to explain limpingly.

"Oh, that was it?" inquired The Thinking Machine curiously as if some question in his own mind had been settled. "What is Madame du Chastaigny's correct name?"

"She iss der famous Mademoiselle Fanchon, und I am der marvellous midget, Count von Fritz," proclaimed Mr. Berkerstrom proudly in playbill fashion.

Then a glimmer of what had actually happened flashed through Hatch's mind; he was staggered by the sublime audacity which made it possible. The Thinking Machine arose and opened a closet door at which he had been staring. From a dark recess he dragged out a suit case and from this in turn a small steel box.

"Ah, here is the radium," he remarked as he opened the box. "Think of it, Mr. Hatch. An actual value of millions in that small box."

Hatch was thinking of it—thinking all sorts of things—as he mentally framed an opening paragraph for this whopping big yarn. He was still thinking of it as he and The Thinking Machine, accompanied willingly enough by the little man, entered the cab and were driven back to the scientist's house.

An hour later Madame du Chastaigny called by request. She imagined her visit had something to do with the purchase of an ounce of radium. Detective Mallory, watching her out of a corner of his official eye, imagined she imagined that. The next caller was Professor Dexter. Dumb anger gnawed at his heart, but he had heeded a telephone request. The Thinking Machine and Hatch completed the party.

"Now, Madame du Chastaigny, please," The Thinking Machine began quietly, "will you please inform me if you have another ounce of radium in addition to that you stole from the Yarvard laboratory?"

She leaped to her feet. The Thinking Machine was staring upward with squinting eyes and finger tips pressed together. He didn't alter his position in the slightest at her sudden move, but Detective Mallory did.

"Stole?" exclaimed Madame du Chastaigny. "Stole?"

"That's the word I used," said The Thinking Machine almost pleasantly.

Into the woman's eyes there leapt a blaze of tigerish ferocity. Her face flushed, then the color fled, and she sat down again, perfectly pallid.

"Count von Fritz has recounted his part in the affair to me," went on The Thinking Machine. He leaned forward and took a package from the table. "Here is the radium. Now have you any radium in addition to this?"

"The radium!" gasped the professor incredulously.

"If there is no denial, Count von Fritz might as well come in, Mr. Hatch," remarked The Thinking Machine.

Hatch opened the door. The small man bounded into the room in true theatrical style.

"Is it enough, Mademoiselle Fanchon?" inquired the scientist. There was an ironic touch in his voice.

She nodded dumbly.

"It would interest you, of course, to know how it came out," went on The Thinking Machine. "I daresay your inspiration for the theft came from a newspaper article, therefore you probably know that I was directly interested in the experiments planned. I visited the laboratory immediately after you left with the radium. Professor Dexter told me your story. It was clever. Clever. But there was too much radium, therefore unbelievable. If not true, then why had you been there? The answer is obvious.

"Neither you or anyone else save Mr. Dexter entered that laboratory. Yet the radium was gone. How? My first impression was that your part in the theft had been to detain Mr. Dexter while someone entered the laboratory or else fished out the radium through a window in the glass roof by some ingenious contrivance. I questioned Mr. Dexter as to your precise acts, and ventured the opinion that you had either sneezed or coughed. You had coughed twice—obviously a signal—thus that view was strengthened.

"Next, I examined window and roof fastenings. All were locked. I tapped over the glass to see if they had been tampered with. They had not. Apparently the radium had not gone through the reception room; certainly it had not gone any other way. Yet it was gone. It was a nice problem until I recalled that Mr. Dexter had mentioned a suitcase. Why did a woman on business go out carrying a suitcase? Or why, granting that she had a good reason for it, should she take the trouble to drag it into the reception room instead of leaving it in the carriage?

"Now I didn't believe you had any radium; I knew you had signalled to the real thief by coughing. Therefore I was prepared to believe that the suitcase was the solution of the theft. How? Obviously, something concealed in it. What? A monkey? I dismissed that because the thief must have had the reasoning instinct. If not a monkey, then what? A child? That seemed more probable, yet it was improbable. I proceeded, however, on the hypothesis that a child carefully instructed had been the actual thief."

Open eyes were opened wider. Mademoiselle Fanchon, being chiefly concerned, followed the plain, cold reasoning as if fascinated. Count von Fritz straightened his necktie and smiled.

"I sent a cable to Madame Curie asking if the letter of introduction was genuine and sent Mr. Hatch to get a trace of a child. He informed me that there was no child just about the time I heard from Madame Curie that the letter was genuine. The problem went back to the starting point. Time after time I reasoned it out, always the same way. Finally, the solution came. If not a monkey or a child, then what? A dwarf. Of course it was stupid of me not to have seen that possibility at first.

"Then there remained only the task of finding him. He probably came on the same boat with the woman, and I saw a plan to find him. It was through the driver of the carriage which Mademoiselle Fanchon used. I got his number by phone at the Hotel Teutonic. He gave me an address. I went there.

"I won't attempt to explain how this woman obtained the letter from Madame Curie. I will only say that a woman who undertakes to sell an ounce of radium to a man from whom she intends to steal it is clever enough to do anything. I may add that she and the dwarf are theatrical people, and that the idea of a person in a suitcase came from some part of their stage performance. Of course, the suitcase is so built that the midget could open and close it from inside."

"Und it always gets der laugh," interposed the dwarf, complacently.

After awhile the prisoners were led away.

10
THE MYSTERY OF THE FLAMING PHANTOM

I

Hutchinson Hatch, reporter, stood beside the city editor's desk, waiting patiently for that energetic gentleman to dispose of several matters in hand. City editors always have several matters in hand, for the profession of keeping track of the heartbeat of the world is a busy one. Finally this city editor emerged from a mass of other things and picked up a sheet of paper on which he had scribbled some strange hieroglyphics, these representing his interpretation of the art of writing.

"Afraid of ghosts?" he asked.

"Don't know," Hatch replied, smiling a little. "I never happened to meet one."

"Well, this looks like a good story," the city editor explained. "It's a haunted house. Nobody can live in it; all sorts of strange happenings, fiendish laughter, groans and things. House is owned by Ernest Weston, a broker. Better jump down and take a look at it. If it is promising, you might spend a night there for a feature story. Not afraid, are you?"

"I never heard of a ghost hurting anyone," Hatch replied, still smiling a little. "If this one hurts me, it will make the story all the better."

Thus attention was attracted to the latest creepy mystery of a small town by the sea which in the past had not been wholly lacking in creepy mysteries.

Within two hours Hatch was there. He readily found the old Weston house, as it was known, a two-story, solidly built frame structure, which had stood for sixty or seventy years high upon a cliff overlooking the sea, in the center of a land plot of ten or twelve acres. From a distance it was imposing, but close inspection showed that, outwardly, at least, it was a ramshackle affair.

Without having questioned anyone in the village, Hatch climbed the steep cliff road to the old house, expecting to find someone who might grant him permission to inspect it. But no one appeared. A settled melancholy and gloom seemed to overspread it. All the shutters were closed forbiddingly.

There was no answer to his vigorous knock on the front door, and he shook the shutters on a window without result. Then he passed around the house to the back. Here he found a door and dutifully hammered on it. Still no answer. He tried it and passed in. He stood in the kitchen, damp, chilly, and darkened by the closed shutters.

One glance about this room and he went on through a back hall to the dining room, now deserted, but at one time a comfortable and handsomely furnished place. Its hardwood floor was covered with dust; the chill of disuse was all-pervading. There was no furniture, only the litter which accumulates of its own accord.

From this point just inside the dining room door, Hatch began a study of the inside architecture of the place. To his left was a door, the butler's pantry. There was a passage through, down three steps into the kitchen he had just left.

Straight before him, set in the wall, between two windows, was a large mirror, seven, possibly eight, feet tall and proportionately wide. A mirror of the same size was set in the wall at the end of the room to his left. From the dining room he passed through a wide archway into the next room. This archway made the two rooms almost as one. This second room, he presumed, had been a sort of living room, but here too was nothing save accumulated litter, an old-fashioned fireplace, and two long mirrors. As he entered, the fireplace was to his immediate left, one of the large mirrors was straight ahead of him, and the other was to his right.

Next to the mirror in the end was a passageway of a little more than usual size which had once been closed with a sliding door. Hatch went through this into the reception hall of the old house. Here to his right was the main hall, connected with the reception hall by an archway, and through this archway he could see a wide, old-fashioned stairway leading up. To his left was a door of ordinary size—closed. He tried it, and it opened. He peered into a big room beyond. This room had been the library. It smelled of books and damp wood. There was nothing here—not even mirrors.

Beyond the main hall lay only two rooms, one a drawing room of generous proportions, with its gilt all tarnished and its fancy decorations covered with dust. Behind this, toward the back of the house, was a small parlor. There was nothing here to attract his attention, and he went upstairs. As he went, he could see through the archway into the reception hall as far as the library door, which he had left closed.

Upstairs were four or five roomy suites. Here in small rooms designed for dressing, he saw the owner's passion for mirrors again. As he passed through room after room, he fixed the general arrangement of it all in his mind, and later on paper to study it, so that, if necessary, he could leave any part of the house in the dark. He didn't know but what this might be necessary, hence his care—the same care he had evidenced downstairs.

After another casual examination of the lower floor, Hatch went out the back way to the barn. This stood a couple of hundred feet back of the house and was of more recent construction. Above, reached by outside stairs, were apartments intended for servants. Hatch looked over these rooms, but they too had the appearance of not having been occupied for several years. The lower part of the barn, he found, was arranged to house half a dozen horses and three or four carriages.

Nothing here to frighten anybody, was his mental comment as he left the old place and started back toward the village. It was three o'clock in the afternoon. His purpose was to learn then all he could of the "ghost," and return that night for developments.

He sought out the usual village bureau of information, the town constable, a grizzled old chap of sixty years, who realized his importance as the whole police department, and who had the gossip and information, more or less distorted, of several generations at his tongue's end.

The old man talked for two hours. He seemed glad to talk and seemed to have been longing for just such a glorious opportunity as the reporter offered. Hatch sifted out what he wanted, those things which might be valuable in his story.

It seemed, according to the constable, that the Weston house had not been occupied for five years since the death of the father of Ernest Weston, present owner. Two weeks before the reporter's appearance there Ernest Weston had come down with a contractor and looked over the old place.

"We understand here," said the constable, judicially, "that Mr. Weston is going to be married soon, and we kind of thought he was having the house made ready for his summerhouse again."

"Whom do you understand he is to marry?" asked Hatch, for this was news.

"Miss Katherine Everard, daughter of Curtis Everard, a banker up in Boston," was the reply. "I know he used to go around with her before the old man died, and they say since she came out to Newport, he has spent a lot of time with her."

"Oh, I see," said Hatch. "They were to marry and come here?"

"That's right," said the constable. "But I don't know when now that this ghost story has come up."

"Oh, yes, the ghost," remarked Hatch. "Well, hasn't the work of repairing begun?"

"Not inside," was the reply. "There's been some work done on the grounds—in the daytime—but not much of that, and I kind of think it will be a long time before it's all done."

"What is the spook story, anyway?"

"Well," and the old constable rubbed his chin thoughtfully. "It seems sort of funny. A few days after Mr. Weston was down here, a gang of laborers, mostly Italians, came down to work and decided to sleep in the house—sort of camp out—until they could repair a leak in the barn and move in there. They got here late in the day and didn't do much that afternoon but move into the house, all upstairs, and sort of settle down for the night. About one o'clock they heard some sort of noise downstairs, and finally all sorts of a racket and groans and yells, and they just naturally came down to see what it was.

"Then they saw the ghost. It was in the reception hall, some of 'em said, others said it was in the library, but anyhow it was there, and the whole gang left just as fast as they knew how. They slept on the ground that night. Next day they took out their things and went back to Boston. Since then nobody here has heard from 'em."

"What sort of a ghost was it?"

"A man ghost, about nine feet high, and he was blazing from head to foot as if he was burning up," said the constable. "He had a long knife in his hand and waved it at 'em. They didn't stop to argue. They ran, and as they ran they heard the ghost a-laughing at them."

"I should think he would have been amused," was Hatch's somewhat sarcastic comment. "Has anybody who lives in the village seen the ghost?"

"No. We're willing to take their word for it, I suppose," was the grinning reply, "because there never was a ghost there before. I go up and look over the place every afternoon, and everything seems to be all right, but I haven't gone there at night. It's quite a way off my beat," he hastened to explain.

"A man ghost with a long knife," mused Hatch. "Blazing, seems to be burning up, eh? That sounds exciting. Now, a ghost who knows his business never appears except where there has been a murder. Was there ever a murder in that house?"

"When I was a little chap I heard there was a murder or something there, but I suppose if I don't remember it nobody else here does," was the old man's reply. "It happened one winter when the Westons weren't there. There was something too about jewelry and diamonds, but I don't remember just what it was."

"Indeed?" asked the reporter.

"Yes, something about somebody trying to steal a lot of jewelry—a hundred thousand dollars' worth. I know nobody ever paid much attention to it. I just heard about it when I was a boy, and that was at least fifty years ago."

"I see," said the reporter.

That night at nine o'clock under cover of perfect blackness, Hatch climbed the cliff toward the Weston house. At one o'clock he came racing down the hill with frequent glances over his shoulder. His face was pallid with a fear which he had never known before, and his lips were ashen. Once in his room in the village hotel Hutchinson Hatch, the weakened young man, lighted a lamp with trembling hands and sat with wide, staring eyes until the dawn broke through the east.

He had seen the flaming phantom.

II

It was ten o'clock that morning when Hutchinson Hatch called on Professor Augustus S. F. X. Van Dusen, The Thinking Machine. The reporter's face was still white, showing that he had slept little, if at all. The Thinking Machine squinted at him a moment through his thick glasses, then dropped into a chair.

"Well?" he queried.

"I'm almost ashamed to come to you, Professor," Hatch confessed after a minute, and there was a little embarrassed hesitation in his speech. "It's another mystery."

"Sit down and tell me about it."

Hatch took a seat opposite the scientist.

"I've been frightened," he said at last, with a sheepish grin, "horribly, awfully frightened. I came to you to learn what frightened me."

"Dear me! Dear me!" exclaimed The Thinking Machine. "What is it?"

Then Hatch told him from the beginning the story of the haunted house as he knew it. He told how he had examined the house by daylight, just what he had found, the story of the old murder and the jewels, the fact that Ernest Weston was to be married. The scientist listened attentively.

"It was nine o'clock that night when I went to the house the second time," said Hatch. "I went prepared for something, but not for what I saw."

"Well, go on," said the other, irritably.

"I went in while it was perfectly dark. I took a position on the stairs because I had been told the . . . the *thing* had been seen from the stairs, and I thought that where it had been seen once it would be seen again. I had presumed it was some trick of a shadow, or moonlight, or something of the kind. So I sat waiting calmly. I am not a nervous man—that is, I never have been until now.

"I took no light of any kind with me. It seemed an interminable time that I waited, staring into the reception room in the general direction of the library. At last, as I gazed into the darkness, I heard a noise. It startled me a bit, but it didn't frighten me, for I put it down to a rat running across the floor.

"But after awhile I heard the most awful cry a human being ever listened to. It was neither a moan nor a shriek, merely a . . . a cry. Then, as I steadied my nerves a little, a figure—a blazing, burning white figure—grew out of nothingness before my very eyes in the reception room. It actually grew and assembled as I looked at it."

He paused, and The Thinking Machine changed his position slightly.

"The figure was that of a man apparently, I should say, eight feet high. Don't think I'm a fool; I'm not exaggerating. It was all in white and seemed to radiate a light, a ghostly, unearthly light, which as I looked, grew brighter. I saw no face to the thing, but it had a head. Then I saw an arm raised and in the hand was a dagger, blazing as was the figure.

"By this time I was a coward, a cringing, frightened coward, frightened not at what I saw, but at the weirdness of it. And then, still as I looked, the . . . the thing raised the other hand, and there in the air before my eyes, wrote with his own finger—on the very face of the air, mind you—one word: *Beware!*"

"Was it a man's or woman's writing?" asked The Thinking Machine.

The matter-of-fact tone recalled Hatch, who was again being carried away by fear, and he laughed vacantly.

"I don't know," he said. "I don't know."

"Go on."

"I have never considered myself a coward, and certainly I am not a child to be frightened at a thing which my reason tells me is not possible, so despite my fright, I compelled myself to action. If the thing were a man, I was not afraid of it, dagger and all; if it were not, it could do me no injury.

"I leaped down the three steps to the bottom of the stairs, and while the thing stood there with upraised dagger with one hand pointing at me, I rushed for it. I think I must have shouted, because I have a dim idea that I heard my own voice. But whether or not I did I—"

Again he paused. It was a distinct effort to pull himself together. He felt like a child; the cold, squinting eyes of The Thinking Machine were turned on him disapprovingly.

"Then the thing disappeared just as it seemed I had my hands on it. I was expecting a dagger thrust, but before my eyes, while I was staring at it, I suddenly saw only half of it. Again I heard the cry, and the other half disappeared. My hands grasped empty air.

"Where the thing had been there was nothing. The impetus of my rush was such that I went right on past the spot where the thing had been, and found myself groping in the dark in a room which I didn't place for an instant. Now I know it was the library.

"By this time I was mad with terror. I smashed one of the windows and went through it. Then from there, until I reached my room, I didn't stop running. I couldn't. I wouldn't have gone back to the reception room for all the millions in the world."

The Thinking Machine twiddled his fingers idly; Hatch sat gazing at him with anxious, eager inquiry in his eyes.

"So when you rushed forward and the thing moved away or disappeared you found yourself in the library?" The Thinking Machine asked at last.

"Yes."

"Therefore you must have run from the reception room through the door into the library?"

"Yes."

"You left that door closed that day?"

"Yes."

Again there was a pause.

"Smell anything?" asked The Thinking Machine.

"No."

"You figure that the thing, as you call it, must have been just about in the door?"

"Yes."

"Too bad you didn't notice the handwriting—that is, whether it seemed to be a man's or a woman's."

"I think, under the circumstances, I could be excused for omitting that," was the reply.

"You said you heard something that you thought must be a rat," went on The Thinking Machine. "What was this?"

"I don't know."

"Any squeak about it?"

"No, not that I noticed."

"Five years since the house was occupied," mused the scientist. "How far away is the water?"

"The place overlooks the water, but it's a steep climb of three hundred yards from the water to the house."

That seemed to satisfy The Thinking Machine as to what actually happened.

"When you went over the house in daylight, did you notice if any of the mirrors were dusty?" he asked.

"I should presume that all were," was the reply. "There's no reason why they should have been otherwise."

"But you didn't notice particularly that some were not dusty?" the scientist insisted.

"No. I merely noticed that they were there."

The Thinking Machine sat for a long time squinting at the ceiling, then asked abruptly, "Have you seen Mr. Weston, the owner?"

"No."

"See him and find out what he has to say about the place, the murder, the jewels, and all that. It would be rather an odd state of affairs if a fortune in jewels should be concealed somewhere about the place, wouldn't it?"

"It would," said Hatch. "It would."

"Who is Miss Katherine Everard?"

"Daughter of a banker here, Curtis Everard. Was a reigning belle at Newport for two seasons. She is now in Europe, I think, buying a trousseau possibly."

"Find out all about her and what Weston has to say, then come back here," said The Thinking Machine as if in conclusion. "Oh, by the way," he added, "look up something of the family history of the Westons. How many heirs were there? Who are they? How much did each one get? All those things. That's all."

Hatch went out, far more composed and quiet than when he entered, and began the work of finding out those things The Thinking Machine had asked for, confident now that there would be a solution to the mystery.

That night the flaming phantom played new pranks. The town constable, backed by half a dozen villagers, descended upon the place at midnight, to be met in the yard by the apparition in person. Again the dagger was seen; again the ghostly laughter and the awful cry were heard.

"Surrender or I'll shoot," shouted the constable, nervously.

A laugh was the answer, and the constable felt something warm spatter in his face. Others in the party felt it, too, and wiped their faces and hands. By the light of the feeble lanterns they carried they examined their handkerchiefs and hands. Then the party fled in awful disorder.

The warmth they had felt was the warmth of blood—red blood, freshly drawn.

III

Hatch found Ernest Weston at lunch with another gentleman at one o'clock that day. This other gentleman was introduced to Hatch as George Weston, a cousin. Hatch instantly remembered George Weston for certain eccentric exploits at Newport a season or so before, and also as one of the heirs of the original Weston estate.

Hatch thought he remembered too, that at the time Miss Everard had been so prominent socially at Newport, George Weston had been her most ardent suitor. It was rumored that there would have been an engagement between them, but her father objected. Hatch looked at him curiously. His face was clearly a dissipated one, yet there was about him the unmistakable polish and gentility of the well-bred man of society.

Hatch knew Ernest Weston as Weston knew Hatch. They had met frequently in the ten years Hatch had been a newspaper reporter, and Weston had been courteous to him always. The reporter was in doubt as to whether to bring up the subject on which he had sought out Ernest Weston, but the broker brought it up himself smilingly.

"Well, what is it this time?" he asked, genially. "The ghost down on the South Shore, or my forthcoming marriage?"

"Both," replied Hatch.

Weston talked freely of his engagement to Miss Everard, which he said was to have been announced in another week, at which time she was due to return to America from Europe. The marriage was to be three or four months later; the exact date had not been set.

"And I suppose the country place was being put in order as a summer residence?" the reporter asked.

"Yes. I had intended to make some repairs and changes there, and furnish it, but now I understand that a ghost has taken a hand in the matter and has delayed it. Have you heard much about this ghost story?" he asked, and there was a slight smile on his face.

"I have seen the ghost," Hatch answered.

"You have?" demanded the broker.

George Weston echoed the words and leaned forward with a new interest in his eyes to listen. Hatch told them what had happened in the haunted house—all of it. They listened with the keenest interest, one as eager as the other.

"How do you account for it?" exclaimed the broker, when Hatch had finished.

"I don't," said Hatch flatly. "I can offer no possible solution. I am not a child to be tricked by the ordinary illusion, nor am I of the temperament which imagines things, but I can offer no explanation of this."

"It must be a trick of some sort," said George Weston.

"I was positive of that," said Hatch, "but if it is a trick, it is the cleverest I ever saw."

The conversation drifted on to the old story of missing jewels and the tragedy in the house fifty years before. Now Hatch was asking questions by direction of The Thinking Machine; he himself hardly saw their purport, but he asked them.

"Well, the full story of that affair, the tragedy there, would open up an old chapter in our family which is nothing to be ashamed of," said the broker frankly, "still it is something we have not paid much attention to for many years. Perhaps George here knows it better than I do. His mother, then a bride, heard the recital of the story from my grandmother."

Ernest Weston and Hatch looked inquiringly at George Weston, who leaned over the table toward them. He was an excellent talker.

"I've heard my mother tell of it, but it was a long time ago," he began. "It seems though, as I remember it, that my great-grandfather who built the house was a wealthy man, as fortunes went in those days, worth probably a million dollars.

"A part of this fortune, say about one hundred thousand dollars, was in jewels, which had come with the family from England. Many of those pieces would be of far greater value now than they were then, because of their antiquity. It was only on state occasions, I might say, that these were worn—once a year perhaps. Between times the problem of keeping them safely was a difficult one, it appeared. This was before the time of safe-deposit vaults. My great-grandfather conceived the idea of hiding the jewels in the old place down on the South Shore, instead of keeping them in the house he had in Boston. He took them there accordingly.

"At this time one was compelled to travel down the South Shore, below Cohasset anyway, by stagecoach. My great-grand father's family was then in the city, as it was winter, so he made the trip alone. He planned to reach there at night, so as not to attract attention to himself, to hide the jewels about the house, and to leave that same night for Boston again by a relay of horses he had arranged for. Just what happened after he left the stagecoach, below Cohasset, no one ever knew except by surmise."

The speaker paused a moment.

"Next morning my great-grandfather was found unconscious and badly injured on the veranda of the house. His skull had been fractured. In the house a man was found dead. No one knew who he was; no one within a radius of many miles of the place had ever seen him.

"This led to all sorts of suppositions, the most reasonable of which—and the one which the family has always accepted—was that my great-grandfather had met someone who was stopping there that night as a shelter from the intense cold, that this man learned of the jewels, that he had tried robbery, and that there was a fight.

"In this fight the stranger was killed inside the house, and my great-grandfather, injured, had tried to leave the house for help. He collapsed on the veranda where he was found, and he died without regaining consciousness. That's all we know or can surmise reasonably about the matter."

"Were the jewels ever found?" asked the reporter.

"No. They were not on the dead man, nor were they in the possession of my great-grandfather."

"Is it reasonable to suppose, then, that there was a third man and that he got away with the jewels?" asked Ernest Weston.

"It seemed so, and for a long time this theory was accepted. I suppose it still is now, but some doubt was cast on it by the fact that only two trails of footsteps led to the house and none out. There was a heavy snow on the ground. If none led out, it was obviously impossible that anyone came out."

Again there was silence. Ernest Weston sipped his coffee slowly.

"It would seem from that," said Ernest Weston at last, "that the jewels were hidden before the tragedy and have never been found."

George Weston smiled.

"Off and on for twenty years the place was searched, according to my mother's story," he said. "Every inch of the cellar was dug up; every possible nook and corner was searched. Finally the entire matter passed out of the minds of those who knew of it, and I doubt if it has ever been referred to again until now."

"A search even now would be almost worth while, wouldn't it?" asked the broker.

George Weston laughed aloud.

"It might be," he said, "but I have some doubt. A thing that was sought for twenty years would not be easily found."

So it seemed to strike the others after awhile, and the matter was dropped.

"But this ghost thing," said the broker, at last. "I'm interested in that. Suppose we make up a ghost party and go down tonight. My contractor declares he can't get men to work there."

"I would be glad to go," said George Weston, "but I'm running over to the Vandergrift ball in Providence tonight."

"How about you, Hatch?" asked the broker.

"I'll go, yes," said Hatch, "as one of several," he added with a smile.

"Well, then, suppose we say the constable and you and I?" asked the broker, "tonight?"

"All right."

After making arrangements to meet the broker later that afternoon, he rushed away—away to The Thinking Machine. The scientist listened, then resumed some chemical test he was making.

"Can't you go down with us tonight?" Hatch asked.

"No," said the other. "I'm going to read a paper before a scientific society and prove that a chemist in Chicago is a fool. That will take me all evening."

"Tomorrow night?" Hatch insisted.

"No. The next night."

This would be on Friday night, just in time for the feature which had been planned for Sunday. Hatch was compelled to rest content with this, but he foresaw that he would have it all with a solution. It never occurred to him that this problem, or indeed that any problem, was beyond the mental capacity of Professor Van Dusen.

Hatch and Ernest Weston took a night train that evening, and on their arrival in the village stirred up the town constable.

"Will you go with us?" was the question.

"Both of you going?" was the counterquestion.

"Yes."

"I'll go," said the constable promptly. "Ghost!" and he laughed scornfully. "I'll have him in the lockup by morning."

"No shooting, now," warned Weston. "There must be somebody back of this somewhere; we understand that, but there is no crime that we know of. The worst is possibly trespassing."

"I'll get him all right," responded the constable, who still remembered the experience where blood—warm blood—had been thrown in his face. "And I'm not so sure there isn't a crime."

That night at about ten o'clock the three men went into the dark, forbidding house and took a station on the stairs where Hatch had sat when he saw the thing—whatever it was. There they waited. The constable moved nervously from time to time, but neither of the others paid any attention to him.

At last the thing appeared. There had been a preliminary sound as of something running across the floor, then suddenly a flaming figure of white seemed to grow into being in the reception room. It was exactly as Hatch had described it to The Thinking Machine.

Dazed, stupefied, the three men looked as the figure raised a hand, pointing toward them, and wrote a word in the air—positively in the air. The finger merely waved, and there floating before them were flaming letters in the utter darkness. This time the word was, *Death*.

Faintly, Hatch, fighting with a fear which again seized him, remembered that The Thinking Machine had asked him if the handwriting was that of a man or woman; now he tried to see. It was as if drawn on a blackboard, and there was a queer twist to the loop at the bottom. He sniffed to see if there was an odor of any sort. There was not.

Suddenly he felt some quick, vigorous action from the constable behind him. There was a roar and a flash in his ear; he knew the constable had fired at the thing. Then came the cry and laugh—almost a laugh of derision. He had heard them before. For one instant the figure lingered and then before their eyes faded again into utter blackness. Where it had been was nothing. Nothing.

The constable's shot had had no effect.

IV

Three deeply mystified men passed down the hill to the village from the old house. Ernest Weston, the owner, had not spoken since before the thing appeared there in the reception room, or was it in the library? He was not certain. He couldn't have told. Suddenly he turned to the constable.

"I told you not to shoot."

"That's right," said the constable, "But I was there in my official capacity, and I shoot when I want to."

"But the shot did no harm," Hatch put in.

"I would swear it went right through it too," said the constable, boastfully. "I can shoot."

Weston was arguing with himself. He was a cold-blooded man of business; his mind was not one to play him tricks. Yet now he felt benumbed; he could conceive no explanation of what he had seen. Again in his room in the little hotel, where they spent the remainder of the night, he stared blankly at the reporter.

"Can you imagine any way it could be done?"

Hatch shook his head.

"It isn't a spook, of course," the broker went on, with a nervous smile, "but I'm sorry I went. I don't think I shall have the work done there as I thought."

They slept only fitfully and took an early train back to Boston. As they were almost to separate at the South Station, the broker had a last word.

"I'm going to solve that thing," he declared, determinedly. "I know one man at least who isn't afraid of it or of anything else. I'm going to send him down to keep a lookout and take care of the place. His name is O'Heagan, and he's a fighting Irishman. If he and that . . . that . . . *thing* ever get mixed up together . . ."

Like a schoolboy with a hopeless problem, Hatch went straight to The Thinking Machine with the latest developments. The scientist paused just long enough in his work to hear it.

"Did you notice the handwriting?" he demanded.

"Yes," was the reply, "so far as I could notice the style of a handwriting that floated in air."

"Man's or woman's?"

Hatch was puzzled.

"I couldn't judge," he said. "It seemed to be a bold style, whatever it was. I remember the capital D clearly."

"Was it anything like the handwriting of the broker? What's his name? Ernest Weston?"

"I never saw his handwriting."

"Look at some of it then, particularly the capital Ds," instructed The Thinking Machine. Then after a pause, "You say the figure is white and seems to be flaming?"

"Yes."

"Does it give out any light? That is, does it light up a room, for instance?"

"I don't quite know what you mean."

"When you go into a room with a lamp," explained The Thinking Machine, "it lights the room. Does this thing do it? Can you see the floor or walls or anything by the light of the figure itself?"

"No," replied Hatch, positively.

"I'll go down with you tomorrow night," said the scientist, as if that were all.

"Thanks," replied Hatch, and he went away.

Next day about noon he called at Ernest Weston's office. The broker was in.

"Did you send down your man O'Heagan?" he asked.

"Yes," said the broker, and he was almost smiling.

"What happened?"

"He's outside. I'll let him tell you."

The broker went to the door and spoke to someone, and O'Heagan entered. He was a big, blue-eyed Irishman, freckled and red-headed, one of those men who look trouble in the face and are glad of it if the trouble can be reduced to a fighting basis. An ever-lasting smile was about his lips, only now it was a bit faded.

"Tell Mr. Hatch what happened last night," requested the broker.

O'Heagan told it. He, too, had sought to get hold of the flaming figure. As he ran for it, it disappeared, was obliterated, wiped out, gone, and he found himself groping in the darkness of the room beyond, the library. Like Hatch, he took the nearest way out, which happened to be through a window already smashed.

"Outside," he went on, "I began to think about it, and I saw there was nothing to be afraid of, but you couldn't have convinced me of that when I was inside. I took a lantern in one hand and a re-volver in the other and went all over that house. There was nothing; if there had been, we would have had it out right there. But there was nothing. So I started out to the barn, where I had put a cot in a room.

"I went upstairs to this room—it was then about two o'clock—and went to sleep. It seemed to be an hour or so later when I awoke suddenly. I knew something was happening. And forgive me if I'm a liar, but there was a cat in my room, racing around like mad. I just naturally got up to see what was the matter and rushed for the door. The cat beat me to it and cut a flaming streak through the night.

"The cat looked just like the thing inside the house. That is, it was a sort of shadowy, waving white light like it might be afire. I went back to bed to sleep it off. You see, sir," he apologized to

Weston, "that there hadn't been anything yet I could put my hands on."

"Was that all?" asked Hatch, smilingly.

"Just the beginning. Next morning when I awoke, I was bound to my cot, hard and fast. My hands were tied, and my feet were tied, and all I could do was lie there and yell. After awhile, it seemed years, I heard someone outside and shouted louder than ever. Then the constable come up and let me loose. I told him all about it, and then I came to Boston. And with your permission, Mr. Weston, I resign right now. I'm not afraid of anything I can fight, but when I can't get hold of it . . . well . . ."

Later Hatch joined The Thinking Machine. They caught a train for the little village by the sea. On the way The Thinking Machine asked a few questions, but most of the time he was silent, squinting out the window. Hatch respected his silence and only answered questions. "Did you see Ernest Weston's handwriting?" was the first of these.

"Yes."

"The capital Ds?"

"They are not unlike the one the thing wrote, but they are not wholly like it," was the reply.

"Do you know anyone in Providence who can get some information for you?" was the next query.

"Yes."

"Get him by long-distance phone when we get to this place, and let me talk to him a moment."

Half an hour later The Thinking Machine was talking over the long-distance phone to the Providence correspondent of Hatch's paper. What he said or what he learned there was not revealed to the wondering reporter, but he came out after several minutes, only to re-enter the booth and remain for another half an hour.

"Now," he said.

Together they went to the haunted house. At the entrance to the grounds something else occurred to The Thinking Machine.

"Run over to the phone and call Weston," he directed. "Ask him if he has a motorboat or if his cousin has one. We might need one. Also find out what kind of a boat it is—electric or gasoline."

Hatch returned to the village and left the scientist alone sitting on the veranda gazing out over the sea. When Hatch returned he was still in the same position.

"Well?" he asked.

"Ernest Weston has no motorboat," the reporter informed him. "George Weston has an electric, but we can't get it because it is away. Maybe I can get one somewhere else if you particularly want it."

"Never mind," said The Thinking Machine. He spoke as if he had entirely lost interest in the matter.

Together they started around the house to the kitchen door.

"What's the next move?" asked Hatch.

"I'm going to find the jewels," was the startling reply.

"Find them?" Hatch repeated.

"Certainly."

They entered the house through the kitchen, and the scientist squinted this way and that through the reception room, the library, and finally the back hallway. Here a closed door in the flooring led to a cellar.

In the cellar they found heaps of litter. It was damp and chilly and dark. The Thinking Machine stood in the center, or as near the center as he could stand, because the base of the chimney occupied this precise spot, and apparently did some mental calculation.

From that point he started around the walls solidly built of stone, stooping and running his fingers along the stones as he walked. He made the entire circuit as Hatch looked on. Then he made it again, but this time with his hands raised above his head feeling the walls carefully as he went. He repeated this at the chimney going carefully around the masonry high and low.

"Dear me, dear me!" he exclaimed, petulantly. "You are taller than I am, Mr. Hatch. Please feel carefully around the top of this chimney base and see if the rocks are all solidly set."

Hatch then began a tour. At last one of the great stones which made this base trembled under his hand.

"It's loose," he said.

"Take it out."

It came out after a deal of tugging.

"Put your hand in there and pull out what you find," was the next order. Hatch obeyed. He found a wooden box about eight inches square and handed it to The Thinking Machine.

"Ah!" exclaimed that gentleman.

A quick wrench caused the decaying wood to crumble. Tumbling out of the box were the jewels which had been lost for fifty years.

V

Excitement, long restrained, burst from Hatch in a laugh, almost hysterical. He stooped and gathered up the fallen jewelry and handed it to The Thinking Machine, who stared at him in mild surprise.

"What's the matter?" inquired the scientist.

"Nothing," Hatch assured him, but again he laughed.

The heavy stone which had been pulled out of place was lifted up and forced back into position, and together they returned to the village with the long-lost jewelry loose in their pockets.

"How did you do it?" asked Hatch.

"Two and two always make four," was the enigmatic reply. "It was merely a sum in addition." There was a pause as they walked on, then, "Don't say anything about finding this, or even hint at it in any way, until you have my permission to do so."

Hatch had no intention of doing so. In his mind's eye he saw a story, a great, vivid, startling story spread all over his newspaper about flaming phantoms and a treasure trove—$100,000 in jewels. It staggered him. Of course he would say nothing about it or even hint at it, yet. But when he did say something about it . . . !

In the village The Thinking Machine found the constable.

"I understand some blood was thrown on you at the Weston place the other night?"

"Yes. Blood. Warm blood."

"You wiped it off with your handkerchief?"

"Yes."

"Have you the handkerchief?"

"Perhaps," was the doubtful reply. "It might have gone into the wash."

"Astute person," remarked The Thinking Machine. "There might have been a crime, and you throw away the one thing which would validate it . . . the blood stains."

The constable suddenly took notice.

"Wait here," he said, "and I'll go see if I can find it."

He disappeared and returned shortly with the handkerchief. There were half a dozen blood stains on it, now dark brown.

The Thinking Machine dropped into the village drug store and had a short conversation with the owner, after which he disappeared into the adjoining room at the back and remained for an hour or more until darkness set in. Then he came out and joined Hatch, who had been waiting with the constable.

The reporter did not ask any questions, and The Thinking Machine volunteered no information.

"Is it too late for anyone to get down from Boston tonight?" he asked the constable.

"No. He could take the eight o'clock train and be here about half-past nine."

"Mr. Hatch, will you wire to Mr. Weston—Ernest Weston—and ask him to come tonight? Impress on him the fact that it is a matter of the greatest importance."

Instead of telegraphing, Hatch went to the telephone and spoke to Weston at his club. The trip would interfere with some other plans, the broker explained, but he would come. The Thinking Machine had meanwhile been conversing with the constable and had given some sort of instructions which evidently amazed that official exceedingly, for he kept repeating "By ginger!" with considerable fervor.

"And not one word or hint of it to anyone," said The Thinking Machine. "Least of all to the members of your family."

"By ginger!" was the response, and the constable went to supper.

The Thinking Machine and Hatch had their supper thoughtfully that evening in the little village hotel. Only once did Hatch break this silence.

"You told me to see Weston's handwriting," he said. "Of course you knew he was with the constable and myself when we saw the thing, therefore it would have been impossible—"

"Nothing is impossible," broke in The Thinking Machine. "Don't say that, please."

"I mean that as he was with us—"

"We'll end the ghost story tonight," interrupted the scientist.

Ernest Weston arrived on the nine-thirty train and had a long, earnest conversation with The Thinking Machine, while Hatch was permitted to cool his heels in solitude. At last they joined the reporter.

"Take a revolver by all means," instructed The Thinking Machine.

"Do you think that necessary?" asked Weston.

"It is. Absolutely," was the emphatic response.

Weston left them after awhile. Hatch wondered where he had gone, but no information was forthcoming. In a general sort of way he knew that The Thinking Machine was to go to the haunted house, but he didn't know when; he didn't even know if he was to accompany him.

At last they started, The Thinking Machine swinging a hammer he had borrowed from his landlord. The night was perfectly black. Even the road at their feet was invisible. They stumbled frequently as they walked on up the cliff toward the house, dimly standing out against the sky. They entered by way of the kitchen, passed through to the stairs in the main hall, and there Hatch indicated in the darkness the spot from which he had twice seen the flaming phantom.

"You go into the drawing room behind here," The Thinking Machine instructed. "Don't make any noise whatever."

For hours they waited, neither seeing the other. Hatch heard his heart thumping heavily; if only he could see the other man. With an effort he recovered from a rapidly growing nervousness and waited. Waited. The Thinking Machine sat perfectly rigid on the stair, the hammer in his right hand, squinting steadily through the darkness.

At last he heard a noise, a slight nothing; it might almost have been his imagination. It was as if something had glided across the floor, and he was more alert than ever. Then came the dread misty light in the reception hall, or was it in the library? He could not say. But he looked with every sense alert.

Gradually the light grew and spread, a misty whiteness which was unmistakably light, but which did not illuminate anything around it. The Thinking Machine saw it without the tremor of a nerve; saw the mistiness grow more marked in certain places; saw these lines gradually grow into the figure of a person, a person who was the center of a white light.

Then the mistiness fell away, and The Thinking Machine saw the outline in bold relief. It was that of a tall figure, clothed in a robe, with head covered by a sort of hood, also luminous. As The Thinking Machine looked he saw an arm raised, and in the hand he saw a dagger. The attitude of the figure was distinctly a threat. And yet The Thinking Machine had not begun to grow nervous; he was only interested.

As he looked, the other hand of the apparition was raised and seemed to point directly at him. It moved through the air in bold sweeps, and The Thinking Machine saw the word *Death*, written in air, luminously swimming before his eyes. Then he blinked incredulously. There came a wild, fiendish shriek of laughter from somewhere. Slowly, slowly the scientist crept down the steps in his stocking feet, silent as the apparition itself, with the hammer still in his hand. He crept on toward the figure. Hatch, not knowing the movements of The Thinking Machine, stood waiting for something. He didn't know what. Then the thing he had been waiting for happened. There was a sudden loud clatter as of broken glass, the phantom and writing faded, crumbled up, disappeared, and somewhere in the old house there was the hurried sound of steps. At last the reporter heard his name called quietly. It was The Thinking Machine.

"Mr. Hatch, come here."

The reporter started, blundering through the darkness toward the point whence the voice had come. Some irresistible thing swept down upon him, a crashing blow descended on his head, vivid lights flashed before his eyes. He fell. After a while from a great distance it seemed, he heard faintly a pistol shot.

VI

When Hatch fully recovered consciousness it was with the flickering light of a match in his eyes—a match in the hand of The Thinking Machine, who squinted anxiously at him as he grasped his left wrist. Hatch, instantly himself again, sat up suddenly.

"What's the matter?" he demanded.

"How's your head?" came the answering question.

"Oh," and Hatch suddenly recalled those incidents which had immediately preceded the crash on his head. "Oh, it's all right, my head, I mean. What happened?"

"Get up and come along," requested The Thinking Machine tartly. "There's a man shot down here."

Hatch arose and followed the slight figure of the scientist through the front door and toward the water. A light glimmered down near the water and was dimly reflected; above, the clouds had cleared somewhat, and the moon was struggling through.

"What hit me anyhow?" Hatch demanded as they went. He rubbed his head ruefully.

"The ghost," said the scientist. "I think probably he has a bullet in him now—the ghost."

Then the figure of the town constable separated itself from the night and approached.

"Who's that?"

"Professor Van Dusen and Mr. Hatch."

"Mr. Weston got him all right," said the constable, and there was satisfaction in his tone. "He tried to come out the back way, but I had that fastened as you told me, and he came through the front way. Mr. Weston tried to stop him, and he raised the knife to stick him. Then Mr. Weston shot. It broke his arm, I think. Mr. Weston is down there with him now."

The Thinking Machine turned to the reporter.

"Wait here for me, with the constable," he directed. "If the man is hurt, he needs attention. I happen to be a doctor; I can aid him. Don't come unless I call."

For a long while the constable and the reporter waited. The constable talked with all the bottled-up vigor of days. Hatch listened impatiently; he was eager to go down there where The Thinking Machine and Weston and the phantom were.

After half an hour the light disappeared, then he heard the swift, quick churning of waters, a sound of a powerful motorboat maneuvering, and a long body shot out on the waters.

"All right down there?" Hatch called.

"All right," came the response.

There was again silence, then Ernest Weston and The Thinking Machine came up.

"Where is the other man?" asked Hatch.

"The ghost. Where is he?" echoed the constable.

"He escaped in the motorboat," replied Mr. Weston, easily.

"Escaped?" exclaimed Hatch and the constable together.

"Yes, escaped," repeated The Thinking Machine, irritably. "Mr. Hatch, let's go to the hotel."

Struggling with a sense of keen disappointment, Hatch followed the other two men silently. The constable walked beside him, also silent. At last they reached the hotel and bade the constable, a sadly puzzled, bewildered and crestfallen man, good night.

"By ginger!" he remarked, as he walked away into the dark.

Upstairs the three men sat, Hatch impatiently waiting to hear the story. Weston lounged back; The Thinking Machine sat with finger tips pressed together, studying the ceiling.

"Mr. Weston, you understand, of course, that I came into this thing to aid Mr. Hatch?" he asked.

"Certainly," was the response. "I will only ask a favor of him when you conclude."

The Thinking Machine changed his position slightly, readjusted his thick glasses for a long, comfortable squint, and told the story from the beginning, as he always told a story. Here it is:

"Mr. Hatch came to me in a state of abject, cringing fear and told me of the mystery. It would be needless to go over his examination of the house and all that. It is enough to say that he noted and told me of four large mirrors in the dining room and living room of the house, and that he heard and brought to me the stories in detail of a tragedy in the old house and missing jewels, valued at a hundred thousand dollars or more.

"He told me of his trip to the house that night and of actually seeing the phantom. I have found in the past that Mr. Hatch is a cool, levelheaded young man, not given to imagining things which are not there. Therefore I knew that anything fraudulent must be clever, exceedingly clever, to bring about such a condition of mind in him.

"Mr. Hatch saw, as others had seen, the figure of a phantom in the reception room near the door of the library, or in the library near the door of the reception room. He couldn't tell exactly. He knew it was near the door. Preceding the appearance of the figure he heard a slight noise which he attributed to a rat running across the floor. Yet the house had not been occupied for five years. Rodents rarely remain in a house—I may say never—for that long if it is uninhabited. Therefore what was this noise? A noise made by the apparition itself? How?

"Now, there is only one white light of the kind Mr. Hatch described known to science. It seems almost superfluous to name it. It is phosphorus, compounded with Fuller's earth and glycerine and one or two other chemicals, so it will not instantly flame as it does in the pure state when exposed to air. Phosphorus has a very pronounced odor if one is within, say, twenty feet of it. Did Mr. Hatch smell anything? No.

"Here we have several facts, these being that the apparition in appearing made a slight noise; that phosphorus was the luminous quality; that Mr. Hatch did not smell phosphorus even when he ran through the spot where the phantom had appeared. Two and two make four; Mr. Hatch saw phosphorus, passed through the spot where he had seen it, but did not smell it, therefore it was not there. It was a reflection he saw. A reflection of phosphorus. So far, so good.

"Mr. Hatch saw a finger lifted and write a luminous word in the air. Again he did not actually see this; he saw a reflection of it. This first impression of mine was substantiated by the fact that when he rushed for the phantom a part of it disappeared, first half of it, he said, then the other half. So his extended hands grasped only air.

"Obviously those reflections had been made on something, probably a mirror as the most perfect ordinary reflecting surface. Yet he actually passed through the spot where he had seen the apparition and had not struck a mirror. He found himself in another room—the library—having gone through a door which that afternoon he had himself closed. He did not open it then.

"Instantly a sliding mirror suggested itself to me to fit all these conditions. He saw the apparition in the door, then saw only half of it, then all of it disappeared. He passed through the spot where it had been. All of this would have happened easily if a large mirror, working as a sliding door, and hidden in the wall, were there. Is it clear?"

"Perfectly," said Mr. Weston.

"Yes," said Hatch, eagerly. "Go on."

"This sliding mirror, too, might have made the noise which Mr. Hatch imagined was a rat. Mr. Hatch had previously told me of four large mirrors in the living and dining rooms. With these, from the position in which he said they were, I readily saw how the reflection could have been made.

"In a general sort of way, in my own mind, I had accounted for the phantom. Why was it there? This seemed a more difficult problem. It was possible that it had been put there for amusement, but I did not wholly accept this. Why? Partly because no one had ever heard of it until the Italian workmen went there. Why did it appear just at the moment they went to begin the work Mr. Weston had ordered? Was the purpose to keep the workmen away?

"These questions arose in my mind in order. Then as Mr. Hatch had told me of a tragedy in the house and hidden jewels, I asked him to learn more of these. I called his attention to the fact that it would be a queer circumstance if these jewels were still somewhere in the old house. Suppose someone who knew of their existence was searching for them, believed he could find them, and wanted something which would effectually drive away any inquiring persons, tramps or villagers, who might appear there at night. A ghost? Perhaps.

"Suppose someone wanted to give the old house such a reputation that Mr. Weston would not care to undertake the work of repair and refurnishing. A ghost? Again, perhaps. In a shallow mind this ghost might have been interpreted even as an effort to prevent the marriage of Miss Everard and Mr. Weston. Therefore Mr. Hatch was instructed to get all the facts possible about you, Mr. Weston, and members of your family. I reasoned that members of your own family would be more likely to know of the lost jewels than anyone else after a lapse of fifty years.

"What Mr. Hatch learned from you and your cousin, George Weston, instantly, in my mind, established a motive for the ghost. It was possibly an effort to drive workmen away, perhaps only for a time, while a search was made for the jewels. The old tragedy in the house was a good pretext to hang a ghost on. A clever mind conceived it, and a clever mind put it into operation.

"Now, what one person knew most about the jewels? Your cousin George, Mr. Weston. Had he recently acquired any new information as to these jewels? I didn't know. I thought it possible. Why? On his own statement that his mother, then a bride, got the story of the entire affair direct from his grandmother, who remembered more of it than anybody else—who might even have heard his great-grandfather say where he intended hiding the jewels."

The Thinking Machine paused, shifted his position and then went on: "George Weston refused to go with you, Mr. Weston, and Mr. Hatch, to the ghost party, as you called it, because he said he was going to a ball in Providence that night. He did not go to Providence; I learned that from your correspondent there, Mr. Hatch; so George Weston might possibly have gone to the ghost party after all.

"After I looked over the situation down there it occurred to me that the most feasible way for a person, who wished to avoid being seen in the village, as the perpetrator of the ghost did, was to go to and from the place at night in a motorboat. He could easily run in the dark and land at the foot of the cliff, and no soul in the village would be any the wiser. Did George Weston have a motorboat? Yes, an electric one, which runs almost silently.

"From this point the entire matter was comparatively simple. I knew—the pure logic of it told me—how the ghost was made to appear and disappear; one look at the house inside convinced me beyond all doubt. I knew the motive for the ghost—a search for the jewels. I knew, or thought I knew, the name of the man who was seeking the jewels; the man who had fullest knowledge and fullest opportunity; the man whose brain was clever enough to devise the scheme. Then, the next step was to prove what I knew. The first thing to do was to find the jewels."

"Find the jewels?" Weston repeated with a slight smile.

"Here they are," said The Thinking Machine, quietly.

And there before the astonished eyes of the broker, he drew out the gems which had been lost for fifty years. Mr. Weston was not amazed; he was petrified with astonishment and sat staring at the glittering heap in silence. Finally he recovered his voice.

"How did you do it?" he demanded. "Where?"

"I used my brain, that's all," was the reply. "I went into the old house seeking them where the owner, under all conditions, would have been most likely to hide them, and there I found them."

"But . . . but . . ." stammered the broker.

"The man who hid these jewels, hid them only temporarily, or at least that was his purpose," said The Thinking Machine irritably. "Naturally he would not hide them in the woodwork of the house, because that might burn; he did not bury them in the cellar, because that has been carefully searched. In that house there is nothing except woodwork and chimneys above the cellar. Yet he hid them in the house, proven by the fact that the man he killed was killed in the house, and that the outside ground, covered with snow, showed two sets of tracks into the house and none out. Therefore he did hide them in the cellar. Where? In the stonework. There was no other place.

"Naturally he would not hide them on a level with the eye, because the spot where he took out and replaced a stone would be apparent if a close search were made. He would, therefore, place them either above or below the eye level. He placed them above. A large loose stone in the chimney was taken out, and there was the box with these things."

Mr. Weston stared at The Thinking Machine with a new wonder and admiration in his eyes.

"With the jewels found and disposed of, there remained only to prove the ghost theory by an actual test. I sent for you, Mr. Weston, because I thought possibly, as no actual crime had been committed, it would be better to leave the guilty man to you. When you came, I went into the haunted house with a hammer—an ordinary hammer—and waited on the steps.

"At last the ghost laughed and appeared. I crept down the steps where I was sitting in my stocking feet. I knew what it was. Just when I reached the luminous phantom, I disposed of it for all time by smashing it with a hammer. It shattered a large sliding mirror which ran in the door inside the frame, as I had thought. The crash startled the man who operated the ghost from the top of a box, giving it the appearance of extreme height, and he started out through the kitchen, as he had entered. The constable had barred that door after the man entered, therefore the ghost turned and came toward the front door of the house. There he ran into and struck down Mr. Hatch, and ran out through the front door, which I afterwards found was not securely fastened. You know the rest of it; how you found the motorboat and waited there for him; how he came there, and—"

"Tried to stab me," Weston supplied. "I had to shoot to save myself."

"Well, the wound is trivial," said The Thinking Machine. "His arm will heal up in a little while. I think then, perhaps, a little trip of four or five years in Europe, at your expense, in return for the jewels, might restore him to health."

"I was thinking of that myself," said the broker, quietly. "Of course, I couldn't prosecute."

"The ghost, then, was—?" Hatch began.

"George Weston, my cousin," said the broker. "There are some things in this story which I hope you may see fit to leave unsaid, if you can do so with justice to yourself."

Hatch considered it.

"I think there are," he said finally, and he turned to The Thinking Machine. "Just where was the man who operated the phantom?"

"In the dining room beside the butler's pantry," was the reply. "With that pantry door closed he put on the robe already covered with phosphorus, and merely stepped out. The figure was reflected in the tall mirror directly in front, as you enter the dining room from the back, from there reflected to the mirror on the opposite wall in the living room, and thence reflected to the sliding mirror in the door which led from the reception hall to the library. This is the one I smashed."

"And how was the writing done?"

"Oh, that? Of course that was done by reversed writing on a piece of clear glass held before the apparition as he posed. This made it read straight to anyone who might see the last reflection in the reception hall."

"And the blood thrown on the constable and the others when the ghost was in the yard?" Hatch went on.

"Was from a dog. A test I made in the drug store showed that. It was a desperate effort to drive the villagers away and keep them away. The glowing cat and the tying of the watchman to his bed were easily done."

All sat silent for a time. At length Mr. Weston arose, thanked the scientist for the recovery of the jewels, bade them all good night and was about to go out. Mechanically Hatch was following. At the door he turned back for the last question.

"How was it that the shot the constable fired didn't break the mirror?"

"Because he was nervous and the bullet struck the door beside the mirror," was the reply. "I dug it out with a knife. Good night."